# Flowers
# In Her
# *Heart*

a novel by
Kellyn Roth

Cover design by Cover Culture
Interior design by Wild Blue Wonder Press
Interior formatting by The Glory Writers

Kellyn Roth, Author
Wild Blue Wonder Press
3680 Browns Creek Road
The Dalles, OR, 97058
www.kellynrothauthor.com

PRESS

*For my dear Trash Can, with friendly regards and a cruel wish that Mr. Mug Man may someday grow facial hair.*

# Prologue

*French Riviera*
*October 1939*

Adele Kee squeezed her daughter's shoulders as her husband's silver car parked outside the train station. Even after he stepped out and reached for the two suitcases in the back, she remained seated, her arms around Judy.

She'd never been so frightened in her life.

Troy circled around the car and set their baggage on the ground. "We need to hurry or you'll miss the train. You have to make this one." His voice was robotic, and she could tell the words pained him.

They pained her, too. She didn't want to leave. Not

so many years ago, with a much smaller Judy tucked in her arms and a single suitcase containing enough of her possessions to travel with, she'd boarded a train at the same station and left. It had taken so much work to reverse the effects of that careless decision when she'd made the decision to return over a year ago. Now she was running again, this time to protect herself, and Judy, and her unborn child from the ravages of war.

At last, Adele released Judy's shoulders and slid out of the passenger side. Troy seemed to understand her slow, choppy movements; he pulled her into a gentle embrace, pressed a kiss to her cheek, his close-clipped reddish mustache brushing there for a moment, then released her.

"It's going to be all right. I promise. I'll follow in a few weeks."

She didn't reply. There was too much fear in her heart—and, above all, the desire to demand that he come with them. That he give up the idea of "battening down the hatches" at their home and with their finances. His promises meant nothing; he couldn't control the tides of war, the movements of nations. He was just one man, and he was her man, and it wasn't fair that he stay behind when she scurried off to the safety of England.

But he wouldn't come, even if she pleaded with him. The set of his jaw and the glint of those pale blue eyes told her so. Troy took care of things that belonged to him. That was his way, and if an entire advancing army couldn't change his course, how could one woman?

"You don't think you'll be delayed, do you?" she

asked for the hundredth time. "It'll only be two or three weeks." *You promised we'd do this together. Don't leave me alone with your children. I won't do this without you again. I won't!*

"I'm sure, Della." He spoke her pet name in a sort of wistful way, one she didn't like—one that hinted of 'I won't say it again for a while.' Over-dramatic, given that in all positive scenarios he'd be with her in a few weeks? Yes. But war was one of the things that made Adele feel over-dramatic. It would a risky beast to play with—a wolf the devoured all in its wake, leaving pain and destruction where it didn't outright kill. Yet Troy was optimist. "We'll keep them off until then."

Adele disliked thinking of the war in terms of "we" and "them," yet here Troy was, bringing it up again. She didn't want to think of the war at all. She hated war more than anything on earth. It was the only thing she knew which had caused more problems to her life than she did.

She couldn't blame her husband for the need for a hasty flight, however. This war hadn't been as forecasted as it should have been, and they had felt they'd be safe to remain in France for a few more months. She supposed they had a neglectful government to blame for that.

Adele wouldn't be bitter. No, no. She mustn't be. She wouldn't think of thousands upon thousands of graves, of the men who hadn't come home from the Great War when she was a child. She wouldn't even think of her two brothers and her father lying somewhere beneath

3

French fields—somewhere that, when Troy had taken her early that year, she hadn't been able to identify exactly. She'd go mad if she thought of that; she would. It was better to ignore the reality of their situation as long as possible, to keep soldiering on even in the face of uncertainty. Perhaps, even, to dare reality to be brighter than her fears.

It wasn't worth considering that this war could be as horrid and brutal as the last. No, it mustn't be. She couldn't lose anyone else, and it seemed like when wars got as nasty as the last one, everyone lost a few people. She didn't know of any untouched families—there was always someone missing, lost, *gone.*

*Just don't let my lost be Troy. Please. I need him.* She wasn't sure if that was a prayer or a simple wish; both options were equally futile. Despite her determination to remain positive, Adele felt the concept of hope was overrated, and she had little to hold on to that would promise a positive outcome. She didn't deserve any favors from the world at large anyways.

She glanced at her husband as he led her and Judy up the train platform. Silently, Adele acknowledged that she had more to lose now than she ever had before.

Her first love had been her brother Kenneth— entirely platonic, of course, but he'd been her first and only thought throughout her childhood, and the main source of her grief from that point forward. Unfortunately, Troy was starting to catch up to her heart, so long reserved in its entirety for a dead relation who she was starting to lose memories of, and overtake

4

her in a gentle, unassuming sort of way. She'd never expected him to take her heart away—not in any real way, in any *lasting* way. Not only that, but she could lose a beloved father of her child—children, come next spring.

Perhaps Adele would play this pregnancy off like an accident when she saw her mother. She didn't want to admit that she could've avoided having this baby—that, in some ways, they had planned their second child. He'd been so happy when she agreed to leave the option open and then when she told him, and, at the time, she'd assumed she'd have his full support throughout the pregnancy.

Adele gritted her teeth. *Marvelous. Absolutely marvelous.* If Troy didn't get out of France, she'd be alone in England with a seven-year-old girl and a baby coming. She'd have to rely on her mother, and her mother would be so smug, so self-satisfied. Mother would assume the baby proved her archaic belief that all women were made for motherhood. Adele wasn't, but perhaps she was made to be Judy's mother. In her opinion, being 'made to be a mother' was something different entirely.

"I want you to go straight to your mother." Troy's voice broke through her scattered thoughts as he urged her to take a seat on a platform bench. Of course the next words out of his mouth confirmed the difficulty that lay ahead—that she would be forced to engage in due to the simple fact that she'd happened to be born. "You might not care for her, but that will give you a place to stay where I know you and Judy will be safe."

"I thought I'd go to Millie." Millie Lark had been her best friend since she was seven and would doubtless welcome Adele and Judy to her flat for a few weeks. Besides, then she could avoid telling her mother she was in London at all until she thought of a way to tell her she'd purposefully not mentioned her pregnancy to avoid having to explain it. Yes, that would do nicely. She'd ease into the subject in time, when she was ready.

"No." His voice was oddly firm for a man who usually gave in to her every desire in a fevered sort of way. "I don't like that you're traveling while expecting, and I want you to go somewhere where someone knows something about babies."

"Hmm." Adele thought she could manage fine, especially since four months wasn't the most troublesome period of a pregnancy, but she wouldn't argue with him. The poor dear didn't deserve it; he only wanted to take care of her.

"Just promise me." His tone was pleading, and those blue eyes were turning puppy-dog on her. "I'll die of worry if I don't know you're safe."

How could she refuse that? She might not exactly love her husband, and she might have only come back to him after a divorce of six years because of Judy, but she wasn't heartless. Not exactly, anyway. She liked him; she respected him; she found him attractive ... and as such, more difficult to resist than she would've preferred.

"All right. I'll do it." She sighed. "But I won't like it. My mother and I will kill each other—and then you'll see how *safe* it is." He'd certainly come back to a house in uproar. Thankfully, Troy could slide into the role of peacemaker when he chose to do so, and he was ever called to play middle-man when it came to Adele and her mother.

Troy smiled. "Thank you." He squeezed her hand. "I'll take care of baggage, and by then it'll be time to get on the train."

As he walked off, Adele sat on the bench, her arm around Judy and her purse clutched in her other hand.

"Are we going to Paris first, Mother?" Judy asked.

"I don't know. I don't think so—and if we do, we won't stop." Adele played with her daughter's hair then dropped her arm. "Perhaps I should see where your father's got to."

"He's been gone two minutes is all." Judy slipped her small, cool palm in Adele's and squeezed. Adele glanced down at her daughter and saw understanding. She smiled but didn't know how convincing it could possibly be. *I'm not a good mother. A good mother would be reassuring. A good mother—*

Troy was back then, his arrival cutting off the harshness of her thoughts. He put an arm around her and his hand on Judy's shoulder as he led them to the train and got them tucked into a compartment.

"I'll see you in a few weeks. It won't be long. Really, Della—don't you worry about it for a moment."

An idle command. He should know better than to ask that of her. "I'll worry about it for a great deal longer than a moment, trust me." She shook her head. "Please

7

be careful. We need you. All three of us do. So follow us soon."

He half-smiled and left the compartment. She watched him go in silence, holding Judy's hand tightly in her own.

As the train left the platform behind, Adele let Judy stick her head out the window and wave, but she didn't look back herself.

She couldn't think of the *what if*s. It would be all right. He would get through. He must.

# Part 1: Durant

"I wish, as well as everybody else, to be perfectly happy; but, like everybody else, it must be in my own way."

~*Sense & Sensibility* by Jane Austen

# Chapter One

*Surrey, England*
*Spring 1940*

It was a beautiful spring day, the kind with birds singing, plants sprouting, and soft, fluffy clouds drifting across a blue sky. The green hills had shaken off the snow and were spotted with trees, rocks, and spotted dairy cattle, and the air was fresh and new.

Somewhere, far away from this sanctuary, a civilian city was being relentlessly attacked. However, there was time to worry about that later—much, much later. For now, Adele watched the hills roll by and admired the child in her arms by turn. When she glanced at Troy, she found him smiling at her.

"How's she doing?"

Adele exhaled a half-laugh, determined not to disturb her daughter. "Fine. Just as fine as she was a few minutes ago when you asked last."

"That's good." He returned his eyes to the road again. "Glad to be going home?"

"Rhetorical questions, dear. Never my favorite." But of course she was glad he was here, glad they were taking their new baby girl back to the small cottage they'd settled in after Troy got them out of London a few months ago.

She caught sight of their cottage around the bend and took Troy's hand. It was overgrown with various vegetation; Adele assumed her mother had been too busy with the nursery to attack the great outdoors. Not that Mother was ever much of a gardener. Adele was the flower-lover of the family.

In that way, at least, there was much to do. Once she had rested a bit more, she could make the house beautiful for the extent of their stay—which, ideally, would be short. Until then, though, she wanted to experiment in homemaking. Maybe she could build something lovely here, something that she hadn't really begun to do in France. Then, when they were truly home at the vineyard, those skills would ideally transfer over.

Adele kissed her baby daughter's forehead and smiled at her husband again. Yes, it was going to be all right. This was home for now, and Troy was here. The war rumbled in far-off cities—or far *enough* off—and Adele was determined not to let it affect her too personally, even if she must feel a distant empathy for those hurt. It wouldn't hurt her; just those around her. It wouldn't.

Not like last time.

Judy Kee sat at the top of the stairs, leaning forward slightly as she watched the door. She wasn't allowed to go outside and potentially dirty her clothes, Granny being sure that she would. Still, she was ready to jump up at any second, ears perked for the car Daddy had borrowed from a neighbor, the last of the petrol being used to provide Mother a safe trip to and from the hospital.

Judy ran her hand through her hair in an imitation of her father's gesture, bumping the blue ribbon tied around her strawberry-blonde locks to the side. She had managed to keep her dress relatively unwrinkled, though, and her shoes weren't scuffed, so Granny's campaign for a nice-looking girl was at least partially successful.

"How much longer?" Judy called up the stairs to her grandmother who was preparing the nursery with the help of her father's sister, Aunt Lola.

"It's a long drive from the hospital. Why don't you come help me set up this room? Come see the things your father bought. He's spoiling his little girl already."

Judy shook her head. "I'll stay here."

She was going to be eight in a month or so, and an eight-year-old really should help her grandmother, but ... She looked longingly at the door. If the stairway was as close as she could get to running all the way to the hospital, then here she'd stay.

Finally, Judy heard the longed-for put-put-put of the old car. She rushed down to stand at the foot of the stairs, bouncing on her toes. "Granny! Granny, they're here!"

Granny swept down the stairs followed by Aunt Lola. "Then you may greet them."

Judy opened the door and rushed out.

Daddy opened the car door and helped Mother to her feet with extra care.

"Really, Troy. I'm perfectly all right," Mother said, glaring at him.

Judy cringed. Sometimes Mother didn't exactly understand what it meant to be loved on.

Daddy smiled easily. "I know, I know. But if a man can't spoil his children because they're likely to be made rotten by such treatment, then whom can he spoil but his wife?"

"You're not spoiling. You're smothering." Mother adjusted her child in her arms and pressed a kiss to the top of her head.

Daddy shrugged, apparently not convinced. "Let me take her for you."

"No. I'll carry her home," Mother said. "Please get my suitcase."

Daddy frowned. "You're sure?"

"Oh dear, I don't know. I might faint halfway up the path." Mother laughed. "Don't worry."

"Daddy! Mother!"

They turned at the sound of her voice. Judy ran down the walk and barreled into Daddy's legs. He swung her around before setting her down and snatching up the suitcase. "Judy, you're gorgeous right now. Let's get inside."

Judy beamed at the praise. She wanted to be hugged more, especially since Daddy had been gone so much these last two weeks and Mother hadn't been home at all, but she supposed there'd be time for that later.

"Yes. The wind might blow me away." Mother pretended to stagger.

"Careful, Della! She's so small, and you're not holding her tightly enough. And you know that's not it. Though you probably shouldn't—"

"Shush, Troy."

Judy tugged at her sleeve. "Mother, may I see? May I hold her?"

"Not yet, Judy," Mother said with a tight smile. She walked quickly toward the house, and Judy sighed. She wanted to see the baby, that was all. Surely there was time for a big sister to meet her new sibling.

Once they were inside the house, Judy couldn't help but ask again. "Mother, now?"

"Patience, Judy."

"But—"

"Don't bother your mother." For the first time since they'd finally become a family again, Daddy's voice held an edge.

Judy swallowed. A rush of tears suddenly escaped from her eyes, but she scrunched up her face and blinked rapidly, keeping the rest at bay. She wouldn't cry like a baby—even if it hurt.

Vision watery, Judy examined her shoes. She'd scuffed the tip of the left toe as she ran outside. This brought more tears. What a bad girl she was!

Granny and Aunt Lola were both allowed to hold the baby and look at her and ask why they'd named her what they'd named her—Camilla Estelle Kee, quite a title for such a little creature. Judy listened to them explaining how her mother had wanted to name the child after her dearest friend, Judy's Auntie Millie, and her full name, Camilla, had supplied. "Estelle," Adele said, "was Troy's choice."

Daddy smiled. "My mother's name."

Oh, right. Her grandmother. The other one she'd never met because she'd died a long time ago from the influenza. Judy wondered why they didn't name *her* after anyone special. Judith was just a plain old ordinary name that anyone could be called. Even her middle name, Ann, wasn't special.

Not like Camilla, who was so special Judy couldn't even hold her. Judy turned and left the room.

Troy looped his arm around Adele's shoulders as

they sat on the sofa. The living room of the cottage was small but cozy, and everyone who belonged there was there. Adele, Mrs. Collier, and Lola, his younger sister.

Lola made soft little cooing noises as she adjusted the baby in her arms. "She's absolutely precious! I couldn't be prouder of my newest niece. Look at all that dark hair!"

"It's quite striking on a baby." Troy thought she was one of the two prettiest infants he'd ever seen. She was like Judy, but also different, and he prayed every day that Camilla's eyes would turn from murky gray to brown. He loved having a little twin in Judy—though he supposed she resembled his sister more—but having a child that looked like Adele would thrill him to the bone.

"I honestly can't believe she's mine, even though I know she is. Judy didn't have a bit of hair when she was born." Adele turned to Mrs. Collier. "Also, Mother, you were wrong when you said I wouldn't miss the anesthetic. I thought I was dying."

Troy glanced out the window, extraordinarily uncomfortable. He hated to think of Adele in pain, and though it had been her decision, he couldn't help a trace of guilt. She hadn't wanted to be a mother again nearly as much as he'd wanted to have another child with her.

Mrs. Collier looked up from her knitting with a forbearing smile. "Of course you did. That's childbirth."

Troy gulped. *Well, then.* Time for another fight. That was just what they needed.

Adele folded her arms across her chest. "But if you knew—"

"I don't want my grandchildren drugged, Adele."

Adele sighed and ran a hand over her eyes. "Serves me right for believing you, I suppose. I know you think I ought to experience it or whatever."

Mrs. Collier cocked her head. "Is it so unreasonable to assume that a woman would want to be at least partially aware when she gives birth? This way you got to hold Camilla when she was new and needed her mother."

"Yes, well." Adele shrugged. "It's not like the hospital let me, anyway."

Troy could see her trying to continue being angry with her mother while truly the experience had touched her. She'd told him as much a few days ago—she'd been glad to be awake, even if she hated the entirety of the experience. He couldn't help but laugh aloud. Adele punched him in the arm without even glancing his way.

"It would be different if the anesthetic didn't put you under." Mrs. Collier set her knitting in her basket with a determined clink as the needles hit each other.

Adele started to respond, but Lola spoke up.

"I think I'd like to be aware. Besides, I read something about it not being best for babies." She kissed the tip of Camilla's nose. "What an angel! How much did she weigh, Adele?"

That was his sister—making sure everyone got along no matter what. He knew she was struggling with jealousy and guilt. Lola had had several miscarriages throughout her married life, and that never stopped hurting. Yet still, she was determined to keep the peace.

As Adele and Lola chatted about the baby's weight, length, and eating habits, Troy settled back on the sofa, an arm looped over the back where Adele's shoulders rested, and watched.

This was his family, from his darling Adele to his new daughter to his treasured sister. Even Mrs. Collier was becoming dear to him—a practical but contained woman. She wasn't always easy to get along with, but he loved her all the same. He hoped some day there'd be healing between Adele and her mother.

Adele certainly needed all the love she could get.

Which reminded him of someone who loved Adele very much indeed. He glanced around the room. Where was his oldest daughter?

"We all would have loved to have Millie here, but she simply can't leave her work, especially now that it's so important to the war effort," Adele was saying. "But she'll come down when she can. Except for Troy, we're a house full of women!" She nudged his arm and smiled up at him.

But he didn't want to discuss the merits of having his mother-in-law and sister stay with them for the duration of the war. It was safer for them both here—both because of the air raids and because here, fresh produce was easier to find.

"Where's Judy?" She didn't often wander off.

Adele's eyes flickered about the room. "Could she have gone to the kitchen? Or outside—I know she loves the countryside, and it's quite lovely today."

"Oh." Perhaps that was it. Though it didn't sound

right.

Adele bit her lip. "It's strange to have Judy wander off, especially since she was so eager to see Camilla."

"I'll go see if I can find her." Troy stood. "Then I'll have to drag that old mattress into the nursery until we can sort something else out. It will do for Judy."

"All right. I'll get Camilla's bottle. Send Judy to the kitchen if you find her; she can help me."

Troy left the room and went to the back of the house. He stepped out of the back door into the tangled mess of a garden. He sighed. He wasn't always a particularly orderly person, but he loved having things nice and neat—and this was decidedly not nice and neat.

Yes, there was a nice patch he'd cleared for vegetables—he'd even started planting some seedlings. But the rest of it he wouldn't have time for. Judy would be left alone to tend their little Victory Garden.

Troy hadn't told Adele about his plans as of yet, and quite honestly, he was afraid to. He knew it would hit her hard. But it had to be done. It was his duty and his honor.

Gritting his teeth, he walked through the long wet grass to the side gate that led out of the garden to the country road. It squeaked and swayed on the hinges but held firm. Small mercies.

Troy had believed settling his family in the country, away from the air raids, was the only way to keep them safe. He still believed country living was safest but wished he'd had time to shop a bit more.

The cottage was far from ideal. It could be lovely, but

it needed so many repairs, and three women, a child, and a baby couldn't very well make them. His brother-in-law, Dave, was already off at war, so that left Troy—and he wouldn't be there much longer, either.

He stepped out into the lane and looked either way, then continued up it to a wooded area. He had an idea where she'd gone—down to a slow brook that ran behind the house. It was peaceful there, and Judy liked peace.

Indeed, there she sat on the bank with her knees up to her chest. A little waterfall fell over the rocks, and Troy could see the appeal. He'd sit there watching the water for hours, too, if he had the time.

"Judy?"

She glanced over her shoulder. "Hello, Daddy. How are you?"

"I'm fine." He walked over and took a seat next to her. "How are you?"

Judy shrugged. "I don't know. I wanted to hold Camilla, but I guess I'm too little. Mother didn't want me to. Neither did you."

"Oh, baby." Troy put his arm around his daughter and squeezed her shoulder. "That's not true! Come back to the house now, and you can help give Camilla her bottle." He kissed her cheek. "You're not too little. You'll be a wonderful, helpful big sister."

Judy grinned up at him. "Really?"

"Yes, really." He stood and helped her up. "Now run home. Your mother should be preparing Camilla's bottle now."

*Flowers In Her Heart*

# Chapter Two

Although Adele wasn't a cook, she enjoyed the light, cheery kitchen. Now, with bottles to prepare and wash and prepare again, it seemed she would be spending plenty of time there.

She tested the heat of the bottle by dripping a little of the formula on her wrist, then questioned the use of the wrist for this important investigation. The door opened after she'd finished dripping hot milk on her forehead, palm, and tongue—a very unsatisfactory experiment.

"Mother?"

Adele glanced at Judy before picking up a rag and washing herself. "Mm?"

Judy eased the back door shut. Her nose was

wrinkled in that adorable confused way. "What are you doing?"

Adele smiled and tossed the damp cloth back in the lukewarm dishwater. "Um, getting Camilla her bottle."

"I thought mothers fed their babies like cats," Judy said, folding her arms over her chest and staring at her mother.

Adele's heart squeezed in an odd way. That was what a good mother would have done—breastfed her child. She felt it was rather barbaric, and it wasn't the current medical recommendation either, but it was one of those things that, if he'd been given a voice on the subject, Troy would have encouraged.

Perhaps someday she'd be strong enough to give up herself so completely that she wouldn't mind being the sole caretaker of an infant. For now, that was a distant, foreign thought. She appreciated the idea of independence even though she was determined to be more involved in the day-to-day feeding and care than she'd been with Judy. There would be no Millie now to hand the baby off to, and her pride wouldn't allow Mother or Troy's sister to spend too much time caring for Camilla.

As for Troy himself ... She'd like him to do some things, but she admitted she couldn't quite trust a man to do much unsupervised.

Adele struggled with words for a minute before blurting out, "Sometimes, and sometimes they bottle feed them."

Judy considered this then nodded slowly. "Like a

sick little lamb?"

"Yes, like a sick little lamb, only perhaps a little less out of necessity and more out of convenience." Adele dried the bottle and set it on the counter. "Where were you?"

Judy smiled. "Outside."

*Just outside? Are we playing the one-word game, then?* "Where outside?"

"By the creek." Judy shuffled her feet and dropped her eyes. "Daddy came and got me. Then we checked on the garden. That's where Daddy is now. We're going to plant vegetables for the war. I rake it every day. Mother, how does planting vegetables help the war?"

"It's about creating our own resources." She hesitated, not sure how to explain to a seven-year-old things she honestly never thought about. "This way we'll have nice, fresh vegetables ourselves, and the men at the front, who can't grow them, will be able to take the ones we would've bought. See?"

"Yes." Judy nodded solemnly. "I'm glad to help. I'd like it to be over. Then we can go back to France and see Harrington and Holt, and Uncle Dave can come back. Right?"

"Right." At least she hoped Dave Cole would return to England. There were no promises in war. There was no solidarity. Anything might happen to anyone.

Adele wished she'd been as strong as the other women in England, but the air raids had been tearing her apart. She was glad Troy brought their family out of London.

Putting on a brave face for Judy and Troy and her mother was exhausting. How she hated war! This was how she'd lost her father and brothers—especially her dearest, darling Kenny. Now the war invaded her country, threatened her home, her child, her husband ... no, it was too much. All too much.

After a few weeks of the raids and the sirens and the shaking ground, she'd wanted to run screaming out into the streets, come what may. It was better than huddling in a bunker, wondering if there'd be a home to return to after it was over.

But no. She wouldn't think of it. She'd move on with her life and pretend there wasn't a war. "Let's go feed Camilla, baby."

"Us?"

Adele reached her hand out to her daughter. "Yes, us! You said you would help lots, didn't you?" *I want to do this right, and I desperately need help.* She didn't say that aloud, however. Troy insisted Judy must not be placed in a position of responsibility for anything Adele did. She understood the sentiment.

Judy beamed. "I just thought you didn't want me helping after all. But Daddy said you did. I like Camilla an awful lot, or at least I'd like to like her. I didn't know if you wanted me."

Adele set the bottle down and leaned back against the counter. "Now, Judy, you should know better than that. Of course I want you! I always want you."

"Sometimes I think you do." She left the words 'and sometimes I think you don't' unsaid, but Adele still heard them.

Judy's words hurt, but she understood. It took a long time to earn trust, and she had done nothing to earn it. "I know what you mean. Sometimes I don't know the things I thought I did either."

*Don't know what I want. Even more accurately, don't know what I need, what is best for me and my family. What a messy world it is—and how insane we act in it.*

Judy smiled, and Adele breathed a sigh of relief. They could still be friends. And she was so desperate to be Judy's friend.

Judy soon settled on the sofa with her little sister cradled in her arms, her parents on either side of her. Granny and Aunt Lola were preparing a meal in the kitchen, so the four were left on their own for the time being.

She looked up at her mother and wrinkled her nose. "Daddy said the nurses wouldn't let him touch the baby at all, and they wouldn't let me come see her. Why do you think they were so mean?"

Mother put her hand under Judy's arm and adjusted Camilla so she rested more comfortably and safely. "It's their job."

Daddy snickered.

She smiled. "Oh, you know what I mean. It's hospital

policy. For safety reasons. Babies can get sick easily."

Daddy pretended to scowl. "That woman had clearly never been a father."

Mother reached over and slapped his arm. At first, Judy was a bit worried—hitting wasn't good—but her mother didn't seem too angry, at least not really.

"What? She hadn't!" He was laughing, though, and it made Judy grin.

Mother shook her head. She frowned, though her eyes were sparkling. "You don't know when to stop, do you? Do you honestly think you're entertaining?"

Daddy brought his hand to his heart and faked a long face. "Judy, did you hear what she said to me? I'm hurt. I am very hurt."

Judy cast him a sympathetic smile, patting his hand consolingly. She'd play along as long as they were only teasing. "Mother, leave Daddy alone."

Mother laughed aloud and nudged her daughter's shoulder. "Judy, I'm disappointed in you. You should know a fool when you see one."

"My poor feelings." Daddy sighed. "I think I need some chocolate, Judy."

She perked up at that. Chocolate was always a good idea. "I think so, too."

"It's almost dinnertime," Mother said.

"Judy and I are rebelling against dinner." Daddy flipped his hand about to dismiss the notion. "We find it a silly habit."

"Oh?"

"Yes. You feel the same way; you never eat anything."

"I need to lose weight. Especially since this little package has arrived." Mother gestured toward Camilla.

Judy sighed. Her mother always thought she needed to lose weight, when really she was the prettiest woman in the world.

"You've been saying that for as long as I can remember, and still you don't eat." His eyes had darkened slightly, meaning teasing was over. He meant what he said now. "You hardly weigh a thing, and, as I've said on numerous occasions, you're starting to feel like a skeleton. Besides, food is necessary to survival."

Mother reached to stroke Camilla's cheek. It was a while before she answered, but when she did, she looked up with a grin. "Yes, but not chocolate."

His face lightened again, and Judy breathed easier. "*Au contraire!* But I won't discuss this with such a chocolate-hater as yourself."

"I can't win, which makes this an excellent opportunity for me to exit stage right and see if Mother and Lola need any help." She made sure Judy was holding Camilla correctly then kissed Judy's cheek. "Thank you for taking such good care of her."

"That's all right. I like to." Judy kept her eyes glued on Camilla's face. "She's a pretty baby."

"She is indeed." Mother squeezed Judy's shoulder and left the room.

Camilla's bottle was about finished, and she fussed and squirmed in Judy's lap.

"There you go. She's finished." Daddy scooped Camilla up and cradled her against his shoulder. "Now,

29

hand me that cloth there. You know why you have to burp a baby, Judy?"

"Gas bubbles," Judy said gravely. Like Daddy, she'd spent a lot of time learning the ins and outs of babies in the past months. She liked being well-prepared, and it was something they could do together.

"Yes, indeed. It'll give Camilla a dreadful tummy ache if we let it stay there." He adjusted Camilla so she rested more comfortably. "See? We could also hold her between my knees or ... hmm, on her belly in my arms. I like holding her like this because she's close to me— closer to me than down on my knees where I can't see her face as well."

As Daddy patted Camilla's back, Judy cocked her head to watch her baby sister. "Does she have blue eyes, Daddy?"

"Not necessarily. She does now—kind of milky gray, anyway. But that doesn't mean they'll always be blue. They could turn brown. They probably will. Look how dark her hair is!" He brushed his hand over Camilla's head so her abundant fluff stood upright. "She's got quite a little bush up there. Never seen a baby with so much hair. It's almost terrifying."

"Terrifying?" Judy placed a hand on his arm and squinted at the baby's head. Her throat squeezed in an odd, sick way. She would hate for anything to happen to Camilla.

But Daddy grinned. "Yes. Why, who knows where hair will sprout next! Maybe she'll develop a mustache like me."

Judy's hand wandered to her upper lip. *It can't be!* "Do ... do mustaches pass on to children? Like hair color or that sort of thing?"

He made a choking sound. "No, baby. Girls generally don't have mustaches. I was teasing."

Judy sighed. That was good. She didn't think she'd look right with one.

Troy and Lola were silent as they walked down the lane between the budding, blossoming trees. He knelt slightly and scooped up a handful of rosy petals, tossing them her way. Lola laughed and brushed the blossoms off her head and shoulders but didn't attempt to start another war.

He guessed she was growing up, which caused him to smirk. He didn't intend to do so himself. At least, he wouldn't grow up in the little ways—he still wanted to be like a child, exploring and playing in the world for the first time.

So what if he was thirty-three? Youth wasn't just for the young. Thirty-three, in the general scheme of things, was a spring chicken.

"Have you heard from Dave lately?" He knew it might be a little sensitive, but Lola generally could handle those types of things, so he was surprised to see tears in her eyes when, at last, she looked at him.

"No, but I didn't expect to," she whispered. Her face

darkened, and her eyebrows pinched together. "Not for another week, anyway. Longer, perhaps—it takes so long for mail to be sorted during a war."

"Oh." He wasn't sure what to say. Lola was his happy little sprite, always dancing and laughing and playing. This wasn't like her. "Are you ... I mean, do you ... Do you think he's all right?"

"I don't know. I *can't* know." Lola shrugged her shoulders then scuffed her foot along the ground in frustration. "I can't know anything until he's safe in my arms again."

"I'm sure he'll write soon. He's sure to. After all, he loves you." Troy squirmed at the admission. He disliked his brother-in-law greatly, or at least he disliked the fact that Dave Cole was the only man in the world Lola loved and admired more than him. But he wanted Lola to be happy, and Dave inevitably made her happy.

"I wish we'd had a baby." Lola's words were quick, like it hurt to force them out, and she needed to get it over with.

"Someday, perhaps." He was never sure quite how to deal with Lola's miscarriages. It frightened him—that life could be conceived and then lost in a matter of weeks.

"I know it sounds silly, but I prayed for a baby when I knew that Dave would be leaving for war. One last chance, if you will. I got myself worked up so I believed it would happen—but it didn't. I suppose it was foolish."

He swallowed. "Not foolish. Optimistic, but not foolish."

"Perhaps it's best—that I don't have to go through it again. But at the same time, you know I don't want to stop trying. Now I feel as if I'll never have a baby when that's all I've ever wanted outside of Dave."

"Oh, Lola, I'm sure you will." Troy ran a hand over his face. "Even so, there's always adoption."

"Troy." Lola's voice was cutting, as it tended to be when Troy or Dave brought up the possibility of the Coles taking a child to raise who was not their own. "Please." She didn't even attempt a patient smile.

Troy sighed. "I just thought ... maybe it was a possibility."

"It's not like we could do so until Dave comes home, anyway."

Troy agreed with that, but he hoped that Lola would at least open herself to the idea in the meantime. He wanted his sister to be happy. Perhaps a baby would do the trick—even if it were someone else's. Would a niece or nephew that wasn't related to him by blood make him any less an uncle? He thought not.

"But when Dave comes home?" Troy couldn't help but nudge her a bit further.

"Maybe." A smile crinkled around Lola's eyes. "You're persistent. Is being an uncle really all that much of a perk?"

"It is. Can't spoil Judy anymore, or so I'm told, and my guess is that the same applies to Camilla." He winked. "Don't you worry! It will be all right. God's taking care of Dave as well as all of us, and He will never let us down. His will be done."

Lola sighed. "I know that, but it's not worked so well for us before."

Troy put his arm around her shoulders and gave her a quick hug. "But it all worked out for the good."

Her eyes met his, dry but pained. "How, Troy? How did losing our parents work out for the good? How did losing my babies work out for good? And now another war ... What's good about that?"

He tried a few sentences out in his head, but his mind told him to avoid the issue a moment longer. "This isn't like you."

"I know it isn't, but I feel as if it's all come crashing down on me. I've been thinking about *Maman* and Papa a lot lately." Lola took a deep breath. "They were so very dear. Don't ever let me forget how wonderful they were, okay? Honestly, I don't know that I ever quite processed it—I was so young, and it happened so fast. Especially *Maman*. But I think, in my heart, I'm still bitter—angry that I never had proper parents when I needed them most. Especially a mother. I wasn't raised by a woman myself. Do you think ... is that why?"

"Oh, Lola, no! It's not a punishment. It's just a part of this sinful world. Like all death and pain." Troy wanted to pull her into an embrace, to comfort the tears away, but he was afraid—there was a fragility in her he was afraid of breaking. It was just so unlike her. "No, don't you dare blame yourself for this—much less God."

Troy watched as Lola wrung her hands, her face twisted as she tried not to cry. "I don't blame God, really. I don't think so, at least. And I don't blame myself. But perhaps He is protecting me from myself. I don't know a thing about babies, really, and I can barely remember our mother, much less how she interacted with us."

"Oh, sweetheart, no one knows that going in! Adele didn't."

"Yes, but Adele *did* have a mother, even if their relationship wasn't—isn't—ideal." Lola closed her eyes for a moment, resting her hand on the fence post beside her. "It would be nice to be around someone who's had some experience with being a woman."

Troy chuckled. "Can't help you there."

"No, and neither can Harrington or Dave. I make a lot of friends through church and volunteering, but we never get close. So it's you, my husband, and Harrington." Lola wrapped her arms around her middle like a protection against outside forces, and Troy didn't like it. Lola didn't deserve to be frightened. "I sometimes feel detached from other women, I think because I need to think like a man to get on in the world I've created. I couldn't raise a little girl—but what kind of influence am I to a little boy? I don't even realize my own femininity half the time."

"That's ridiculous." In fact, he refused to believe that there was anyone in the world more qualified. "You raised me, didn't you?"

A somewhat humorless chuckle, forced for his benefit, but it was something. "I suppose so."

"Look, you can make friends, right? Maybe the new church here will be nice. I'm sorry I haven't attended with you yet—I'm going to start now that we've got the baby home. There will be dozens of wonderful women who all want to be your best friend, and you can take your pick. And some older, motherly types who will interfere with your life and disagree with all your decisions."

"Is Adele rubbing off on you?" Lola smiled and shook her head. "All right, I'll plan on this wondrous new church changing my life. Though they've been none too friendly as of yet. Are we taking Judy?"

Troy nodded. "Adele will stay home Sunday mornings for a month or so—we agreed on that while we were at the hospital, since she's still not comfortable with church, and I suppose there's a touch of a cold going around the village which she doesn't want Camilla to get. But Mrs. Collier will come."

Lola sighed. "Of course. That woman and her endless chipped shoulder."

"Shush, Lola—you have to live with her now." Troy took her hand. His sister was taller than his wife, but her hands were about as small—they always felt so delicate. "Come on, let's head back. Trust in God, all right? He's not blaming you or punishing you, and you are not under-qualified. You're perfect. But we have to wait for His time; we can't order our own lives."

Lola squeezed his arm. "As always, my big brother knows exactly what to say."

If only that were true. Troy's qualifications for preaching were few indeed—he could only do his best and pray it was good enough for the Lord's purposes.

# Chapter Three

When Millie Lark arrived at the Kee home late Saturday morning, Adele dragged her up the stairs and into her bedroom so they could talk. It had been too long, and this was the first time they'd seen each other since the arrival of Millie's namesake.

As Adele had known she would, Millie adored Camilla. She sat on the edge of the bed just holding her with a look of awe and pride, and Adele's heart crinkled around the edges—a feeling somewhere between pleasure and pain.

That should be the way she looked at her babies—and really, she hoped she did. But she was in the habit of being a bad mother. It was a hard one to break. She loved Judy and now Camilla with all her soul, but at the same time, there was a daily struggle to give up her own wants and needs.

*Millie wouldn't struggle with that if she were a mother. She'd be perfect—always selfless, always loving. She would be the perfect woman, the perfect wife, and yet I'm the one who was given—*

Her thoughts came to an abrupt halt, and she focused her attention on answering Millie's queries about the baby to distract herself from another hard question: *Why was I given this?*

As Millie cooed over the baby some more, Adele's thoughts invaded. *Why? I don't deserve this. I shouldn't be a mother. Other women, more deserving women, are left childless. Millie, Lola ... Yet I am the one entrusted with Judy and Camilla.*

She tried to pretend she didn't believe in a Higher Power, but truly, it would seem that something or someone was directing her life.

"So she sleeps with you, then?" Millie asked. "In this room, I mean, in her basinet."

"Right. It's easier to have her close. She's up every few hours, if she sleeps that much." Adele sat on the bed beside Millie. "Honestly, I don't remember Judy being this bad. She's always been such a quiet creature. Camilla is fussy."

"I think every baby is different. They're people, after all, same as us." Millie shifted the infant onto her shoulder and patted her back. "She's precious. I love how she's got so much hair, and isn't it strange—you'll have a dark-haired child after Judy, our sunshine girl."

"Mm." Adele rested her hand briefly on Camilla's

head. "She is pretty. Troy is so proud of her—he wants to take her to church and show her off, but I said no."

"Oh?" Millie cocked her head. "Why?"

"Because she'll be fussing through the service. It will annoy Mother. Besides, there's a cold going around the village. I'd rather keep her here with me."

"Ah. So you're not going?"

"Not for a month or so. Troy and I negotiated. I hate church—I'll do it for Judy's sake, but if I can get out of it for a few weeks, I'm absolutely taking the opportunity."

Millie kissed the top of Camilla's head, watching Adele warily. "I thought, perhaps, when you remarried Troy that you'd come to a bit of a … a changing place." Hesitantly, her eyes searched Adele's face. "I could see no other reason for such a turnaround."

"It was Judy. I couldn't lose her. Perhaps I might have feelings for Troy. I believe I do." Adele wrung her hands together. "I'm glad now, at least, that we had another baby. I wanted to please him, and it has—pleased him, I mean."

"Hmm." There was a moment of silence before Millie spoke again, "So it's platonic, then? Your marriage?"

Adele coughed. "Obviously it's not platonic." She gestured to Camilla. "And she wasn't the only time we—"

"Right, right." Millie winced. "Sorry. I suppose I was referring more to your emotions. Are you in love with him or is it just friendship?"

Adele raised her eyebrows. "It's sort of friends with benefits."

Millie moaned aloud. "I'm sorry I asked."

She smirked. "Millie, I'm not even using filthy language or anything. You're so innocent."

Millie smiled ruefully. "Sorry."

"Don't be sorry. One of us should be sweet, I think." She reached her hand out and smoothed it over Camilla's head. "She'll need her bottle in a few minutes."

As Adele could have predicted, her friend's eyes glowed. "Oh, that'll be nice."

"Mm, it loses its charm after a few days, trust me." Adele rolled her eyes. "I'm trying my best, Millie, but I'm tired and cranky and ready for the baby stage to be over. And the toddler stage. Honestly, can she be six or seven already?"

Millie chuckled. "I feel the opposite. She's so little and precious now—I never want to give her up. Have I mentioned that I'm beyond honored to have her named after me?"

"Only a thousand times. I'm glad it pleases you." Adele rose. "Troy snapped a couple photos and had them developed yesterday; I want you to take the one of Judy holding Camilla. I love it. He took several of them. I'm having one framed."

"Ah. That'll be nice to have."

As Adele shuffled through a trunk where she'd stuffed the folder of photographs, she heard Millie speak up again behind her.

"Adele?"

"Hmm?"

Camilla began fussing, and Millie whispered

soothing words before asking her question. "Did you skirt my question earlier?"

She pulled out the folder and slid it open. "What question?"

"The one about you and Troy. Are you in love with him?"

Adele pulled out the photograph and stood. "Does it matter?"

Millie was silent as Adele extended the picture of a grinning Judy holding a sleepy Camilla. She accepted it with her free hand before replying. "It doesn't matter, really. It is in you to be faithful and raise his children without any emotions involved. I'm the first to admit that being in love isn't really as important as loving him with your actions. But it does matter, sort of."

Camilla's whimpers became louder, and Adele bent to take her from Millie's arms. "Shush, now. I know you're hungry. Let's go, Millie."

"Adele. Really. Are you going to answer me?"

With Camilla against her shoulder, Adele met her best friend's eyes evenly. "I suppose I care for him more than most. I'm certainly attracted to him. I'm not ... I'm not in love with him in the way I was before. But he makes me feel special, and he's a good father—a good man."

Millie smiled softly. "I suppose that's close enough."

It felt a bit too traditional and stoic for Adele's taste, but she nodded. "Close enough," she repeated in a murmur.

In the kitchen, Adele turned the subject to Millie's

life. She didn't talk about her friend often enough, really. Millie was humble and quiet, and she almost never brought up her own pains—but Adele knew everyone had them, even if they were smothered.

But, always, it was the same report—"Yes, work is fine—busy but fine. Nothing new there. No, no man I'm interested in. I don't think I will meet one, but that's all right. I'm not *trying*, exactly, but goodness, singleness isn't a curse. Oh, I think anyone who lives alone gets lonely, but I visit my parents when I can—I still go to church with your Aunt Ella while I'm with them, by the way, and she sends her love. I have friends at work and church. No, I don't really want to just date; I think I'll wait until I find someone who wants to be serious."

There was such a thing as waiting too long, in Adele's opinion. But to each their own. Millie probably didn't have the constitution for dating. Her heart would be broken; she loved too intensely for casual relationships, even if they were pure.

There was such danger in loving—really loving—someone. But at least Troy and Camilla and Judy were all safe at home with her. Nothing could happen to them.

And past pains couldn't hurt her any more. They wouldn't.

Millie's sister Ruthie had gotten married and had a baby now—and a husband in France, which made Adele wince. Having a husband in France must be like having a brother in France, only worse.

Meanwhile, Millie's other sister Shellie was completely content with her singleness.

Adele rolled her eyes. "Like you're content with it?" she asked drolly.

"No." Millie cocked her head, eyes blinking solemnly behind her spectacles. "She legitimately doesn't want to be married. She's always known she wouldn't marry. But I am content, Adele—I'm just waiting. I'm living in the meantime."

Adele sighed. Millie and her endless waiting for God to provide. "Even you would say God helps those who help themselves."

"There are two sides to that, Adele. Let me tell you—"

As always, Millie took this chance to turn conversation toward more theological zones. Adele humored her, but she wasn't interested in discussing God. Millie might as well give up. God didn't care about Adele. It was a sad but true fact of life. She'd done too many things wrong to merit forgiveness, and anyway, even when she was an innocent child, He had abandoned her.

The wreck of her life, as far as Adele could tell, had happened long before she became a sinner. Which meant, no matter what she did, He didn't care. In fact, perhaps He took a special sort of pleasure in destroying her life.

She didn't voice this to Millie. She smiled, nodded, and said, "That's all very well and good for you, Millie, and for Troy, but not for me. I'm not interested in that."

"Religion or God?" Millie countered.

"Either. Both. I don't know." Adele sighed. "Let's talk

about something else."

Troy played with his collar for the third time in the past few minutes as they walked into the country village. The church bells tolled, meaning he'd estimated the time the walk would take correctly. Good.

He squeezed Judy's hand and offered her a little smile. She returned it, though he thought it wobbled around the edges. Poor dear. She hated meeting strangers. This was probably torture for her. But it was necessary.

Mrs. Collier walked slightly behind him, and without looking, he knew that her shoulders were rigid and her face strict. Proper church behavior. He sighed, doubting that God wanted His congregation to be serious and joyless.

Lola was on his other side, though she was probably daydreaming based on the expression her face held. In another world, thinking about what it might be like to ride a cloud or own a unicorn.

At least, he liked to imagine that was what was going through Lola's mind. She could also be worrying about Dave or obsessing over their parents' deaths and the reasoning behind them.

A shiver went down his spine as he thought about the future. He couldn't leave. Yet his sense of duty and honor forbid him from doing anything less. He owed that much to France, surely, and to his father's memory.

He glanced around the building as they entered it. Attendance was sparse. Half the men gone to war, no doubt—and boys who should never have to set foot on the battlefield as well.

He led his little group to a pew at the back and slid in. Judy climbed into his lap, and he didn't complain though truly she was getting too big. He hugged her close and kissed her forehead.

Lola squeezed his arm. "Isn't this a nice place? But the service doesn't start for ten minutes. I feel like we should socialize instead of just sitting down."

Troy glared at her. "Heaven forbid."

"Oh, come on. It'll be fun." She nudged him with her elbow, grinning. "You're such an old dud."

He rolled his eyes. She could call him what she wanted, but in the end, she would be the one caught in a tortuous conversation with the town busybody—not him. He believed in being pleasant at all times, but he had plenty of friends. Really.

Lola could be best mates with the world if she wanted to. That was her business. As for Troy, he liked to mind his own. Harrington had taught him that.

Lola giggled then pushed away from Troy and turned to Mrs. Collier. "Elizabeth, should we talk to people? Do you know anyone yet?"

"Not really. I met the pastor and his wife." Mrs. Collier shifted the pew, perhaps uncomfortable with Lola calling her by her given name.

Troy loved his mother-in-law—really, he did—and

he understood her need to hold fast to the morals and restrictions she'd been raised under. However, she was terribly stiff sometimes. Troy hoped someday he'd bring a dash of fun and whimsy into her life.

After all, she was one of his own. He thought loyalty included caring about the spiritual and emotional well-being as well as the physical of one's friends.

Now, if only he could convince his Della that he had her spiritual life in mind—and that Jesus Christ was the only One who could make her happy.

But that was a thought for another time. He ignored Lola's chattering and Mrs. Collier's stoic replies and turned his attention to Judy.

"You're quiet," he whispered.

Judy's thin eyebrows raised. "You're supposed to be quiet in a church, Daddy."

He smiled. "We can talk softly until the service starts. Are you tired?"

Judy nodded. "It's early for waking up."

It wasn't, but lately they'd been struggling to keep Judy to a set bedtime with the baby getting them up at odd hours. "It's worth it to spend time with me, right?" He put on a conceited expression, twisting his mouth oddly to make her smother a giggle.

"I think so."

"You think so?" Troy feigned offense. "Well. If that's how you feel about it." He forced himself to become serious. "Baby girl, you know why we're at church?"

Judy's chin jerked up and down dutifully. "Yes. To learn about God."

"Yes, and to meet other Christians." He winced. He wasn't doing such a good job about that—he never had. His focus wasn't on meeting people when he knew a great many amazing people both related to him and not. But that wasn't right.

"Will we meet other Christians?" Judy asked.

Troy sighed. Much as he'd hate it, it was necessary. He wanted to show Judy firsthand what it was to be a Christian in this world. She'd taken a few tentative steps toward salvation—and he wanted to make sure she learned the right things. "Yes, we really ought to. After the service—seems like they're starting."

After the final hymn was sung, Troy and Judy rose with the rest of the congregation.

Lola disappeared almost before they were finished, ready to make new friends, her earlier depression seemingly lost. Mrs. Collier, on the other hand, quietly moved out of the pew, but thankfully, she fell into conversation with another woman around her age.

Good. Troy was going to focus on meeting new people. He grunted. What a difficult task. But Judy shouldn't be a hermit like Harrington—something Troy believed he himself had become for several years.

He wished Adele was here. Someone needed to be the outgoing one. But she would hate this crowd, since they were Christians. He didn't feel that asking her to come to church to protect him from strangers was a good way to get her participating. It might make her even more resentful—and in a month or so, he'd have to force her.

At last, Troy decided to discuss the sermon with the pastor. It'd be something, at least. Thankfully, Judy would still be attending with Lola after he left—and he could trust Lola to be a good Christian. At least in the sense of meeting others.

Of course, it was useless to meet people he might never see again. He swallowed. No. People he wouldn't see again for a period of time. That was much better. But he would at least talk to the pastor.

Holding Judy by her shoulders, he stood at the back of the crowd until it thinned and then went to speak to the man. The preacher was an older, balding gentleman who looked like a stereotypical English clergyman was supposed to look.

He smiled at Troy as he approached, squinting through his spectacles. "I haven't seen you around before, sir." His loud but pleasant voice, just like at the pulpit, made Troy smile.

"I've never been here before." He held out his hand. "I'm Troy Kee, and this is my daughter, Judy."

The clergyman shook Troy's hand and then knelt to shake Judy's, his eyes meeting hers. He was slow to raise from his knees, but he managed it. "It's nice to meet you both! Are you new to town?"

Troy nodded. "We own a cottage a few miles out now. Had to get my family away from London."

The pastor blinked. "Indeed. I'm glad. We have a few young ones staying with us, actually, until their mothers can call them back after it's over. Poor dears are homesick, though my wife does her best."

Troy frowned. It was a shame they had to be separated from their parents, but thank goodness they'd been able to get out of London safely. "I'm glad someone's taking them in."

"Oh, hundreds are—we're one of many." The clergyman scratched the back of his head. "Did you enjoy my sermon? I can't say it was my best. I tend to follow rabbit trails wherever they lead me, as my wife says."

Troy had considered the sermon to be rather dry and, indeed, quite rambly, but he grinned. "Oh, no, not at all! It was nice."

"Good. Will you be coming again?"

Time for a commitment. "Yes. Or at least my sister and Judy will be. And my mother-in-law."

"Ah." The man seemed to understand that no able-bodied fellow under the age of forty was likely to be attending any church in England for very long. "Right. And your wife?" His words were careful, as if he suspected that Troy was a widower. Troy hated to break it to him, but that just wasn't the case. Death was respectable, but at least she was alive, and perhaps, someday, she would attend.

"She's at home with our new baby. They're a bit tired—mother and daughter." That would do for now. No use breaking Adele's reputation right away. Perhaps he'd let Lola do that after he was gone.

"Ah, congratulations! A little girl, is it?"

"Yes, sir. Camilla."

"Good—fine name." The man nodded. "When Mrs.

Kee is recovered, Mrs. Ichabod and I would love to have you and your family over for dinner at our house."

Troy lifted his eyebrows to avoid wincing. "That's very generous, but I'll be leaving soon, I think. I'm going to London this Monday."

He felt Judy's eyes on him; however, he focused in on the clergyman before him. "My prayers will go with you, Mr. Kee. It's a shame that a family man must go. However, I suppose we all must make sacrifices. When I think about the last war ... You were probably too young to remember, but I served. It seems surreal that it's all happening again."

"My father was killed in France." In a war he hadn't wanted to fight, no less. Though Troy wouldn't tell that to this near-stranger. "But we were invaded. I'm half French, and I've lived there since after the first war. I wouldn't have chosen to fight in a war, but it has been chosen for me."

The pastor was not overly enthusiastic about this statement, nor did Troy expect him to be, but Troy felt that he needed to speak his reasonings to someone who couldn't contradict him. He didn't believe Adele would understand.

"We'd best get home before Adele wonders where we've got to." Troy shook the man's hand again. "Thank you for the wonderful sermon."

"Thank you," Judy mimicked, offering a bit of a smile for the first time.

"You're both very welcome." Then the man turned to speak to another congregant, and Troy went to collect

Mrs. Collier and drag Lola away from the other women she was talking to.

Trouble making friends, indeed.

*Flowers In Her Heart*

# Chapter Four

After Troy, Lola, Judy, and her mother returned from church and started making noise in the kitchen, Adele thought it worthwhile to rise from her bed and get dressed.

She'd been up any number of times before to tend to Camilla but otherwise had catnapped most of the morning. She'd been up rather late with Millie before she returned to London around midnight. Then of course Camilla tended to be a baby, which was expected and yet tiring.

At least Camilla wasn't dead yet. Rather a morbid thought, but it was what her mother expected of her—that she'd fail drastically at motherhood and something horrible would happen.

That wouldn't be the case. No, not this time. She'd raise Camilla with love and care, even on the days she didn't feel like it.

They were sitting down to lunch when Adele arrived with Camilla in her arms. Troy rose and helped her get the baby settled in a bassinet by the window.

"She's been fed?" Mother asked, voice icy.

Adele gritted her teeth. "Yes. I've been taking care of her all morning, Mother. You needn't worry."

Mother gave no response.

"You missed a capital sermon from a really pleasant man, Della," Troy said.

Adele rolled her eyes. "I've been in the room three minutes, and already you two have managed to point out a multitude of my sins. Really, Troy! I've been up with Camilla half the night."

"I wasn't trying to point out anything." He smiled. "Here. Mother's gotten us a good meal together, and we should try to enjoy it."

Adele wanted to grouse more, but it was apparent Troy thought he'd made peace. She wouldn't disillusion him just yet, though it would never be exactly peaceful for Mother to live with them. They didn't get along. That was the simple truth.

Adele ate in silence while Troy, Lola, and Judy chatted cheerily with each other and Mother put in an occasional word. She thought, perhaps, that she mildly deserved her mother's judgment, but that didn't make it pleasant or helpful. Adele knew she'd failed Judy for years.

In some ways, the idea that she was a bad mother was rather firmly ingrained into her mind. She woke up in a cold sweat at night, afraid something terrible had happened to one of her girls.

It was worse than worrying about Kenny had been in those terrible months. She hadn't known anything could be worse than that. But she loved Judy and Camilla in a different way. A cleaner, bigger way.

She didn't trust herself because in the past she hadn't shown love toward Judy. Yes, in the deepest part of her heart, there had been distant affection, but she hadn't acted on it. Adele knew now that there was no point in loving with the heart and nothing else.

"What about you, Della?" Troy asked.

Adele looked up from the spoon she was swirling in her practically untouched bowl of stew. "Hmm?"

"Daydreaming?" Troy grinned then repeated his question. "Do you want to go walk down to the village with Judy, Lola, and me? Mother is going to stay and watch Camilla either way. We want to see what there is to see."

"Er, no, thank you." Adele took a determined sip of her soup. "I think I'll curl up and read this afternoon."

"Okay." Troy rose and picked up his plate.

She sat still as the others cleared the table around her. A quarter of an hour later, she finished and carried her bowl into the kitchen. Her mother was there, putting away the last of the dishes.

Adele quietly placed her bowl in the dirty dishwater. "Are they gone?"

"Yes."

"Oh. Good. I'm glad Judy's getting some fresh air."

"Hmph."

Adele suspected her mother cared very much about Judy getting fresh air, but was too stubborn to agree with her daughter.

From the other room, Camilla began fussing, and Adele ran to fetch her. She scooped the baby up and cradled her against her shoulder. She patted and rubbed the infant's back, but her whimpers turned to screams.

"What in heaven's name have you done to the child?" Mother stood in the doorway, hands on her hips.

"Nothing! She's ... I don't know."

"Does she need changed?"

Adele checked. "I don't think so, no."

"All right." Mother crossed the room and held out her arms.

She clutched her daughter close. "What? You don't know what's wrong any more than I do."

"Adele—"

"No! Don't you act like you're the perfect mother." She pressed a kiss to the top of Camilla's head and rocked her body back and forth. "There, darling, it's all right. I've got you," she murmured.

But Camilla's cries grew more urgent, and Mother started forward again. "She must be hungry."

"She shouldn't be; she just ate." Adele was more than willing to argue with her mother at this point. Camilla was her child, and surely, surely she must know what was best for her. Even if she wasn't sure why the baby was screaming her lungs out.

"She has a smaller stomach than you, so she needs to feed more often." Mother's tone was bone dry, and it was obvious she found the whole situation and Adele's incompetence absolutely ridiculous.

"I know that!" Adele snapped.

Camilla belted out a shriek louder than the others and squirmed incessantly.

"Now you're scaring her."

Adele's arms trembled a bit, but she took a seat at the dining room table with Camilla clutched to her chest and tried to control the twitching of her face. She could do this—or rather, there wasn't anything she couldn't do that her mother could. Camilla was her baby, and she would keep her—no matter what.

"She's probably hungry." Mother folded her arms in front of her chest and huffed. "I can't believe you're ignoring her cries."

Adele didn't respond; she just sat there, rubbing Camilla's back. "It's been a quarter of an hour since she ate, and she took most of the bottle then, but if you want to fix her another one, that's fine." Her voice was calmer than she expected.

Mother turned and marched into the kitchen. Shortly after she left, Camilla's screams turned to fussing with occasional louder outbursts. Adele held her through it, murmuring soothing words and snuggled her close. It helped a little but not as well as she would have liked. How she wished she'd appreciated Judy's quiet childhood—she didn't know how good she'd had it!

Camilla wouldn't take the bottle, and in fact grew more tempestuous at having it shoved in her face. Giving her mother a look which Adele only hoped could kill, she stood. "I'm going to see if there's anything itching at her, though I checked before."

"Why don't you let me try?" Mother's face was stony again. Adele supposed she was firmly convinced that she'd have some sort of magic touch that would quiet the baby.

"I think you've *helped* enough."

Mother frowned. "You're preventing me from helping. She's plainly in distress. You've probably gotten her too hot or pricked her with a pin or—"

"I'm sure I'll figure it out, thank you very much." Adele left the room quickly and hurried to her room where she laid Camilla down in her crib. This caused a roar which only turned back to fussy squirming when she was picked up.

"What is it, sweetheart? You poor thing." She pulled out a change of clothes and awkwardly got Camilla out of her romper and clothed her in a different one.

Camilla didn't take kindly to the cold air when her clothing was removed, and the tantrum she threw was the most tempestuous yet. But after about fifteen minutes, she quieted and then fell asleep, albeit with a bit of squirming and twitching.

Adele sat in her chair by the window, still holding her baby, and stared straight ahead of her. Her thoughts were still spinning about rather uselessly. *Could that have been my fault? Was it something I did?*

Judy had been primarily silent when she was small, and Adele might never adjust to the level of volume an infant could produce. Camilla was so tiny to have such wondrous lung capacity, and Adele couldn't figure out what had gotten her started.

Nightmares? Ghosts? Who knew, except Camilla and God. If God even knew.

Troy came up then, and after one look up, asked her what was wrong. It was then Adele realized that she'd been crying.

She ran a hand over her cheeks, dashing away the worst of the tears, and sniffled. "Camilla screamed most of the time you were gone," she whispered. "I don't know why."

"Ah," he breathed. "Is she all right?"

"I think so. I don't … I don't know." She bit her lip. "I don't know what was wrong with her, Troy, and nothing I did—"

"Shh, it's okay! Sometimes babies are fussy like that." He knelt beside her chair and placed a hand on Camilla's back. "She's fine now. Look at her! She's perfect. So are you." He leaned forward and kissed her cheek. "Don't you worry. It's going to be all right. I promise. You're doing great—and we're here to help in any way you need."

"Thanks," Adele said weakly. She didn't feel great by any stretch of the imagination, but if Troy said so maybe she was believable as a mother. "Do you think … I mean, I know I wasn't exactly maternal with Judy. Millie would get up with her a lot, actually, and I didn't."

"Yes, but it's coming to you, I think." He squeezed her shoulder as he stood. "Judy can help you. Just say the word, and there's someone to hold a baby while you go scream in the closet." He winked.

Adele managed a soft chuckle. "I suppose so, if it comes to that."

Troy grinned. "Let's hope you'll survive. I was about to go call Harrington and ask him about sending Holt over, but if you need me to babysit, I'm more than willing."

"No. That's fine. I'll sit for a while longer." She needed some time to calm down, and she didn't feel like she could calm down if Camilla was out of sight, let alone out of her arms.

"Okay, then. Don't worry too much, okay, Della?"

"I won't." Another lie, but what did it matter if she added another supposed sin to the tally? She was beyond saving at this point anyway.

Adele rolled over in bed and opened her eyes. She lay still for a moment, listening, then moaned and tugged the covers over her head.

"What's wrong?" Troy's voice was thick from sleep.

She flipped her arm over her eyes. "I woke up."

"Oh, dear. How will you manage?" Adele could hear the chuckle in his voice, though he kept his tone low, thankfully.

"I didn't want to wake up until Camilla did. She fussed until long after midnight, as you know." It had been an exhausting, frustrating night after an exhausting, frustrating day. As far as she could tell, the baby wasn't colicky or otherwise sick; she was just excessively noisy.

*I'm worried.* She was insanely worried about a tiny baby who was in all likelihood absolutely fine. Motherhood was such a strange, tiring job. And there were women who wanted this?

Troy shifted in the bed beside her, and she felt his arm come around her waist, tugging her close. "At least we know she has a healthy set of lungs and isn't easily tired."

She flapped her arm in his direction in an attempt to ward him off but kept her eyes tight shut. "You keep quiet. I'm going back to sleep."

Troy held her arm down and kissed her cheek. "All right, grouchy." He shifted back. "I'm leaving early today for London."

"London? Why?" Adele asked, rolling over to face him.

"I'm joining the infantry."

It was one of those moments when, for a moment, Adele forgot to breathe. Every muscle in her body went tense, especially the ones in her stomach which tightened abnormally.

"But you can't go, Troy," she said at last. "You should stay with us. Wait until we've settled in. I don't know if I can manage without you."

Troy smiled. "Of course you can. You're stronger than you think, Della."

His faith in her was sweet but sadly unfounded. "I'm not strong. You *know* I'm not strong. Troy, I know you feel an obligation—or patriotism or whatever it is ... pride, I suppose—but you have a *family*. We need to come first."

"I know, Dell." His grin vanished replaced by solemnity, eyes darkening, lips pressed together. "In a perfect world, that would be true. But we're at war. We're far from the perfect world scenario."

"But ... but ..." Adele could think of no other objection. If her own needs and those of their family weren't enough, nothing would be. "I don't want you going off and getting killed. I want you to stay. I want to be with you." *Don't you know I love you a little? Don't you know I've lost everyone who mattered to a war?*

He instantly straightened. "I'm glad of that. But it doesn't change anything. I promise to do my best not to get killed." Troy winked. He was joking now, making light of a serious subject. He didn't want to get hurt, and Adele understood that, but at the same time, this was no laughing matter at all.

"Every man makes that promise. How few keep it?" Adele said. "You know there are no certainties. Besides, you're thirty-three."

His ears turned red. At least he wasn't entirely delusional. "So? Men older than me are signing up. Those who aren't are forming home guards and such. Everyone's giving of themselves. Even women. As nurses or air-raid wardens—anything to free up another man to fight."

"I don't want that man to be you," Adele whispered. "I can't imagine ..." Why he'd need to go. Life without him. Another loss. "And they wouldn't ask it of you, would they? You with a wife and two children?"

"Everyone needs to go beyond the call of duty." Troy sat up and ran his hands through his hair. "It's not an obligation. It's an honor. Who knows what will end up happening? Maybe I'm not considered fit. All I know is I intend to offer my services. They need men who can do other things, too, you know. Still, I have no doubt that I'll end up in the infantry."

Adele rolled back onto her stomach and pulled the covers up. Her throat felt oddly itchy, her stomach clenching. She hadn't felt this way in years.

The worst thing was that this specific feeling was familiar. She'd felt exactly like this when her brothers and father had gone off to war—she a child younger than Judy. Afraid, knowing it was bound to happen no matter what she did, and yet doing everything she could think of to prevent it. She didn't want him to go, but he would. Nothing would keep him.

"Good luck." She cleared her tight throat and ran a hand over her burning eyes. "Just remember to stay safe. And if there's another way—take it."

She felt him sit on the edge of the bed near her and place a hand on her shoulder. "All right, Della. I will."

*Flowers In Her Heart*

# Chapter Five

Troy wasn't sure how to feel when he arrived back at the cottage that evening. His heart was a strange mix of heavy and light that tugged and pulled every organ in his body a different direction.

He was glad he'd enlisted. It was the only option for him, the option he'd known he would take since he was an eleven-year-old boy watching his father march off to fight the Germans. Besides, this war seemed more black and white in terms of the good and the bad. It made the decision all the easier.

But that didn't make war anything less than hell. Not that he'd been in a war before—not exactly. He'd seen the aftermath at close range, lost both his parents, seen the pain in the eyes of the men who returned. Harrington still struggled with a fear of loud noises if they were too sudden or he wasn't completely aware of their origins. He wasn't entirely sure how much of Harrington's general attitude toward life was due to the war—and how much was just his personality.

Troy *was* a bit afraid, as any man should be when facing potential death and at least a few years apart from his loved ones, but he was also proud. He knew he'd made the right decision, and he knew God would be with him.

Adele met him outside the door, arms crossed around her stomach, eyes wide. "Well?" Her tone wasn't accusatory or angry. She sounded resigned. *Poor dear.*

He smiled as he stepped toward her and took her arm. "I've been accepted into the infantry."

"Oh." Still no emotion in those beautiful brown eyes.

He wrapped his arm around her waist. "I'm due to report next week. I have a few weeks of training, and then I'll be sent to France. I don't know all the details yet."

"That soon." Adele's eyes wandered about the horizon and down the road and over the flower pots on the porch—anywhere but up to meet his. "That was what you wanted, I suppose."

He swallowed. "Yes. I'm surprised everything happened so fast. I suppose life speeds up during a war." His life certainly had. Sped up until it spiraled out into nothingness, and he and Lola were alone in the world. Horrid. He prayed God would spare his family that emptiness.

"And at the same time drags on," Adele said. She pulled away from him and straightened a flower pot full of cheerful daffodils. "I remember a bit. I was so little. I don't know if I've just been told stories about the time or if ... if I honestly have memories."

Troy nodded. He was almost sure she did remember but had blocked parts out, as he had. Still, he didn't challenge her. "I'm the same way about some details. I remember being so proud of my father joining the army—and at the same time confused. He waited, you know. Didn't agree with the cause. But it got to the point where he had no choice if he wished to maintain his dignity."

Adele winced. He knew that, like him, her mind went to white feathers and alleyway beatings. "I remember people being cruel. They were hurting so badly; I can hardly blame them. I was angry myself. But morals are morals."

Troy raised his eyebrows, surprised. "Thought you didn't believe in those." Or, at least, they were conditional for her.

She turned to him then. "I do. I really do, Troy. I just have my own system."

That wasn't very comforting. If there was no guiding force deciding what made things moral or immoral, then all was madness. But to each their own, he supposed. He'd cast his lot with Adele, for better or for worse. Someday, perhaps, she would share his beliefs.

Until then, he must be patient. More patient than he

felt like being, definitely.

She cleared her throat. "Still, I don't believe that anyone should try to get people to go against their convictions."

A silence stretched on. Adele knew his feelings on the subject, so he didn't feel a need to reiterate them. Troy was rather tired of endlessly longing for his wife to be something she wasn't.

*Time to lighten the mood.*

Troy put a hand on her shoulder and grinned as broadly as he could manage. "Say I consider it wrong not to have a healthy dose of chocolate each day ..."

Adele rolled her eyes. "You really can't take anything seriously, can you? I'd forgotten, you know. You were so serious, so determined when you came to get Judy. I'd never seen you like that. You scared me, but it wasn't you."

"It was me—a different me. Troy with a plan."

Adele smiled. "What was the plan, exactly? It rather got lost in the shuffle, I think."

He cocked his head. "I only had one thing on my mind, and that was Judy. I couldn't let myself hope for us again. I wanted you to call me back yourself. Not to visit Judy—but for you. I'd finally told myself to stop asking for that. I suppose God knew better than me." He took a deep breath. "And I call my joking a survival technique, Della."

She pulled her bottom lip in, rubbing lipstick off on her teeth. "I don't believe much in 'God knowing better,' but I'm glad you waited until we weren't quite so hurt. I don't know about you, but I think I needed time to grow up."

"I think I'd been grown up for a while, but maybe that's my pride speaking." Troy closed his eyes for a moment. "I don't know. At any rate, we can't stand out here chatting all night. We should tell them." He nodded toward the house.

Adele sighed. "Must we?"

He understood the dread. Sharing this sort of news was never comfortable, and every one in this family had a history with wars. A tragic history. There was a lot of fear to be worked through, especially for Lola and Mrs. Collier. Still, he wouldn't delay. "Yes. We've got to. It's better they know now. Have time to prepare. Don't worry—we've got a lot of tough women in this house."

"Oh?" Adele seemed skeptical of this, and Troy supposed she had seen her mother at her worst. But he believed in the women in his life.

"Mm-hmm." He smiled. "Judy's a little trooper, your mother can take anything short of a joke, and Lola ..." He swallowed. "Let's just say she's used to it. Probably anticipated it. She'll be fine in the end, or she will after an existential crisis or two."

Adele nodded slowly. "All right. Let's go in."

*Two Weeks Later*

Tomorrow was the day for the goodbye.

Judy was going to be eight years old this summer, which was probably too old to cry, even though she hadn't grown any taller since she was seven. But her throat had that itchy, strangled feeling that said, "Tears are coming if you don't watch out!"

She swallowed and smiled extra hard at her father, squeezing his hand in time to their steps.

His steps were bigger than hers, though she was starting to catch up with him. She remembered a few years ago when her legs would run two steps for his every one. Now it was more like one very big step for his every small step.

She did a little skip with a kick at the end of it, just to prove to herself that she wouldn't cry. The sun shone, and a light breeze swayed the branches of the cherry trees above them, causing petals to fall down and rest on their heads and shoulders.

It was beautiful. Judy knelt and picked up a handful and threw them into the air. Her father crouched beside her.

"Isn't God's creation wonderful, baby?" he asked.

Judy nodded. "I think cherry blossoms are my favorite kind of blossoms." Not that she'd seen a lot of blossoms in her life, of course, as a girl who was raised in the city portion of London. Even the French Riviera didn't boast cherry blossoms of this beauty.

She glanced up at her father, since he was taking a while to respond. Was it silly to have a favorite kind of blossom? But he was smiling.

"I agree," he said. "I am partial to apple blossoms because I love apples, but cherries are definitely a favorite. Look! Aren't they a pretty shade? Just like your cheeks." He playfully tugged on one of the pigtail braids bouncing over her shoulder.

Judy tossed her head so her braid flopped onto her back where it belonged. "Thank you," she said because there wasn't much else to say.

They walked on a little further, chatting about this and that. They kept the subject matter light, focused on books they'd read and places they'd like to see. Judy didn't talk about all the things she wanted to do with him.

What if, for any number of reasons, they never got to do those things? Like travel to India and ride elephants together, or see cowboys in the Wild West, or walk along the Great Wall of China until it met the sea?

She wanted so badly to do those things with him. Those marvelous adventures that only her Daddy was a fit companion for. But now it might never happen.

She hated the war. She hated it as much as her mother did now. And nothing, nothing was going to make it all right if it went wrong.

*It's okay,* she told herself. *He's still here, and perhaps nothing bad will happen.*

But bad things seemed to happen so easily in Judy's life, and she was afraid. So, so afraid.

*Oh, God, I only just found my daddy again! Please, not yet.*

She believed God heard that prayer, one of a

thousand she'd uttered lately, but at the same time she knew one didn't get everything one prayed for.

Daddy himself had taught her that. God wasn't a service one paid for in prayers and obedience; He was a loving Father who gave of His grace and mercy freely—and the rest of His ways were beyond comprehension.

"Judy?" Daddy's voice was gentle, but even so, it was jarring to be woken from such deep thoughts.

She blinked up at him. "Yes?"

"Are you okay?"

"Yes." But her voice was heavier than she'd intended, and she was willing to bet her face was all dark and gloomy.

He nodded and didn't say anything else. He just kept walking—off the road and straight up a hill into a cherry orchard.

Overhead, bees buzzed. Normally, Judy was a bit scared of bees, but in this case, she made an exception. She knew she could trust her daddy to take care of her, even if bees were in possession of stingers.

At last they found a big cherry tree with a knotted trunk. They took a seat at the roots, Judy on her father's lap. He kept an arm firmly wrapped around her.

"Judy, tell me something."

"Okay."

"Are you afraid of me being killed in the war?"

Judy swallowed. She'd never lied to her father before—and she didn't exactly want to start now. He was always honest with her, and she liked to return the favor. Also, lying was wrong, even if it was to make someone feel better. No lie was any better than another. They were all big and black, even if people might call them little and white.

She squirmed and wiggled, but the answer had to come out truthful. "I guess." Her voice sounded normal even though her stomach felt like a billion caterpillars had hatched inside and were crawling around.

She squeezed her stomach muscles to get them to stop, but they kept on, regardless of her desire for them to quit and stay still.

"That's what I thought." He leaned back against the trunk of the cherry tree and stretched his arms, yawning loudly in a way that always made her giggle.

But she didn't even smile. Just silently bore the caterpillars in her stomach with her mouth twisted in an effort to hold them in.

"Hmm." He dragged that 'hmm' out indefinitely. "You know, when I was only a few years older than you, my daddy went off to war. And he didn't come back."

Judy swallowed hard and wrapped her arms around herself, closing her eyes tight. The caterpillars had gone from larva or pupa stage, and somehow they'd managed to form one heavy chrysalis at the bottom of her tummy.

It was nauseating and made her feel like a thousand weights were dragging her down. There were also some chrysalises at the back of her eyes and throat and inside her ears.

She blinked rapidly.

"Hmm," he said again. "That's right. He didn't come back. But you know what?"

She couldn't get a word out through all the growing butterflies, so she simply shook her head jerkily.

"God still loved me. He still took care of me. He still treasured me. And nothing ever happens the same way twice. So I may come back to you, Judy. I'm going to do my best to come back. But if I don't, know that I love you, and I will *always* love you, and there is *nothing* you can do to keep me a bit safer except pray and pray and pray."

"But ... but ..." Judy swallowed a thousand times and finally managed to get the words out. "But what if you don't come back?"

And then it happened. All the butterflies burst from their cocoons, and Judy found herself crying and crying into her father's chest, until every last insect had made its way out of her mouth and nose and eyes.

When the last of the butterflies was gone, she lay there, exhausted, and listened to his soft soothing words and felt his gentle back pats and, overall, was quite relieved.

"My stomach feels better," she whispered.

"Was it hurting?"

She nodded.

"I'm glad it's not anymore." He kissed her forehead and smoothed her sweaty hair back from her forehead. "Judy?"

"Yes, Daddy?"

"Whenever you need to cry, you just cry. Don't ever let anyone tell you it's not a strong thing to do or that you'll hurt yourself by doing it or that you need to be brave. It's very brave to cry. Okay?"

"Yes, Daddy."

"Good girl. Now let's get back to the cottage before your mother worries."

# Chapter Six

Love was a funny thing. Sometimes it was big and bright and flashy and obvious. Knees shook, hearts fluttered, pulses raced, and souls swelled with emotion.

Other times, it was quiet. Subtle. It gently stole in while one was sleeping or at odd times when it wasn't expected. Gradually, it wooed, and devotion came over time in an unhurried, gentle way.

Adele couldn't say which was the stronger love, but she knew herself to be firmly gripped by the latter. She'd had the former with so many men, including Troy, but never before had she experienced the second type.

Always for her it was fireworks and bombs going off behind her ears. The attraction, the excitement, the desire for union—and then the burning, the tearing, of the departure. Now it was more like violin music slowly crescendoing but never making it much louder than mezzo forte.

But it was love, and every day of those last two weeks confirmed it. Though perhaps not in love with him, she loved Troy Kee. She loved his smile and his laugh and those blue eyes which showed all his emotions before he had time to hide them.

She loved his sweet, companionable relationship with Judy, and the way he'd coo at Camilla into the wee hours as if it weren't insane to be up that late. She loved his obsession with chocolate. She loved his insistence that his big yellow dog come live with them—and at last Holt was installed in the garage with access to the front yard every few hours.

She would never love his mustache. But life wasn't perfect like that.

Adele was going to miss him. His kisses and hugs, his stupid jokes, his flattery and his honesty, his faithfulness and his care.

And in those last two weeks, she experienced a new emotion. One she would have laughed at if she'd been told it existed. Of course, it wasn't exactly a new emotion—it was more of a mix of old ones blended together in a more intense fashion.

Dread, hope, sadness, love, longing, anger, resignation, jealousy, loyalty, and fear entwined together to make this powerful feeling, and Adele hated it. It was a nasty, beautiful, heavy, light, grieving, hopeful combination.

Adele analyzed it for almost two weeks while she watched Troy play with Judy in the garden, snuggle the latest addition to their family, chat with his sister, flatter her mother, and throw sticks for Holt which inevitably ended up chewed to bits.

At last, she believed she understood what it was. She was experiencing everything a woman ought to feel when her husband went off to war, plain and simple.

Then, with new tenderness, she would turn to her mother and wonder—*Is this what she felt? Is this why she reacted as she did in those terrible days?* And of course the most daring question—*If so, is it in me to forgive her?*

Lately, Adele had more questions than answers.

The day he was to leave, she woke up early. The house was still quiet, but she could tell that Troy was already up beside her.

"Good morning," he whispered.

She scooted over into his arms, and he held her close, pressing her face into the buttons of his pajamas until they left marks on her forehead.

"You know what I'm going to miss most?"

"Mm?"

"I don't either. I've never been to war before."

She punched him in the stomach, and he chuckled softly and took it without complaint.

"I think I deserved that."

"You certainly did." Still, Adele kissed his cheek then hugged him as hard as she could. There wasn't time for everything she wanted, even though it was still early, but she wasn't letting go. Not until she had to.

Then Troy got up and dressed, and she had to get up to tend to Camilla. The house stirred, yawned, and stretched, and it was full of people running around—mostly Judy and Lola, who wanted a last minute with their father or brother, respectively.

Adele gave them their last goodbyes, which they shared through little jokes over breakfast and lingering smiles and hugs.

Shortly after breakfast, they all walked to the train station. They'd long since run out of petrol for the beaten-down car which their neighbors couldn't use anymore either, and it wasn't far. Even Mother came without a word about the extra trip into the village.

There were hugs and kisses and lots of *I love you*'s and *write when you can*'s. He held her longest, and of course he kissed her longest, but in the end, he was as gone from her as from the others.

"I love you so much, my darling. I hope you know I love you more than anyone," were his last words to her, whispered into her ear.

But she chickened out at the last minute and said, "I know," as always. There was disappointment in his eyes; he had wanted more from her. Seconds later, as the train pulled away, she hated herself.

Why hadn't she said it?

But it hadn't seemed right, and Adele was never one to ignore her intuition.

Adele didn't think about it as they walked home.

When they got back to the cottage, she put Camilla down for a nap. Then she laid her head on the pillow of her own bed, pressed her hands to her face, and wept.

Her inner protests of *I'll see him again once or twice before he deploys* and *Just because you lost her brothers and father doesn't mean you'll lose him, too* were useless.

She was scared. She was so terribly scared.

The house smelled of bleach, mold, mopwater, and dust. It had since the day her daddy boarded the train.

Judy's Granny kept the cleaning going, and Aunt Lola eventually joined her. Granny always said that a neat house was necessary to a neat mind, and though Aunt Lola didn't seem to agree, she didn't seem to mind donning an apron and tying up her hair and diving into dust bunnies.

Perhaps it was a nice distraction for her. She seemed pretty sad sometimes.

Judy helped where she could, but she was only a little girl, and more often than not, she was underfoot. Cleaning wasn't her specialty.

They cleaned the kitchen first, and then Granny attacked the parlor. After a rather disastrous episode involving the rarely used, much-blocked fireplace, Judy was told to "run along and play while they finished up."

A bit heartbroken and feeling unwanted, Judy

scurried off to do as she was told. But it was a lonely sort of day, and the heavy rainfall kept her from wandering outside. In the end, she walked into the already-clean kitchen.

To her surprise, her mother was there already, sitting at a chair with a cup of tea and a book. Camilla was in a small basket at her feet which her mother was absently rocking with her toe.

Mother looked up with a smile. "Hello, Judy."

"Hello, Mother."

"Did you get kicked out, too?" She winked conspiratorially, and Judy grinned.

"Yes."

"Oh, dear! We're all in exile to the kitchen together, then. Let me get you some biscuits. You deserve a reward for lasting as long as you did."

Though she didn't quite understand what her mother meant, Judy was glad for a biscuit or three, and she followed her mother to the cupboard.

"Wash your hands first," Mother said as she pulled a tin off the top shelf. "You have soot on them, I think."

Judy glanced down at her hands. Yes, she did indeed. "We were clearing out the fireplace flue."

"Ah, that makes sense."

Judy washed her hands in the sink, dried them carefully, then took the plate of biscuits, tops crusted with cinnamon and sugar, from her mother. "Thank you."

"You're welcome. You must share, though."

Judy raised her eyebrows. "With Camilla?"

"No, silly. With me." Mother laughed. "Camilla can't have any. She's too little. You should know that!"

Judy did know that, but it seemed more reasonable than her mother voluntarily eating anything that could be considered fattening or unhealthy. She was reasonably sure biscuits were both.

But oh well. Hers was not to reason why.

"What are you reading?" Judy asked after a bit.

Mother took a sip of her tea before answering. "Oh, *Emma*. I can't count how many times I've read it, but it always makes me smile. It's a fun book. You'll like it in a few years, I think."

"What's it about?"

"It's about a rich young woman who believes she can make a match—or rather find a husband or wife—for everyone she knows."

"Oh." Judy cocked her head. "Does she?"

"She does—and it all goes horribly wrong. In the end, absolutely no one marries who she intended." Mother smiled and shook her head. "Don't try matchmaking, Judy. It seldom works."

"Okay." Judy wasn't about to try anyway, so it was an easy promise to make. She was of the opinion that very few people with the exception of her parents actually needed to get married. If Aunt Millie got married, for instance, it would mean she wouldn't love Judy as hard.

Judy needed everyone who loved her to love her as hard as they were able.

Mother stood then and went to the window. "I think

the rain is stopping."

"That's nice," said Judy. Though she liked the rain, it did put a damper on walks. She wouldn't have minded going for a walk when the sky was crying, but her mother didn't like her to get wet.

Judy liked walks. They were calming. If she knew where she was going, then it was a familiar ramble over places she loved. And if she didn't, it was an adventure.

"I'm so bored," Mother said, turning to face Judy. Camilla made a soft cooing noise from her basket as if she agreed. "What could we do?"

"We could go outside," Judy said, rising to her knees in her chair and craning her head towards the window behind her mother's back.

Adele shook her head. "Nothing to do outside."

Judy frowned. "We can't leave the kitchen because it smells so bad in there with all the cleaning things Granny and Aunt Lola are using. So perhaps we'd better find something to do outside. I have galoshes. So do you, I think. We could put Camilla somewhere under an umbrella."

Mother laughed. "Judy, we can't put Camilla down anywhere. She's a baby, not a doll. She has to have special care."

"All right. You'll have to carry her, then, until we find a place," Judy said. "I can't carry her. She's too heavy."

"She is a fat little baby." Mother bent over and scooped Camilla up in her arms. "Hello, Camilla."

Judy climbed up on a chair and leaned against her mother, peering down at the baby. "Isn't she pretty?"

"She is, indeed." Mother turned to the door. "Fetch our things, and we'll go."

Judy scampered off to do as her mother said.

They walked together into the damp world and surveyed their surroundings. Adele took a deep, bracing breath of the cool air. It was brilliant, and her mind and heart felt instantly lighter.

She tucked the blanket more carefully about Camilla, afraid the chill would seep through, and stepped forward with Judy at her side.

Troy had cleared out a large patch of weeds, leaving only brown dirt in their place, but the rest of the garden was badly unkempt.

Adele winced. To her, there was no greater ugliness than a neat garden, specifically the one Troy had started with its perfect rows and mounds of dirt, primly groomed with vegetable seedlings peeping up at regular intervals.

The rest of the garden, the tangle of wild, uncontrollable weeds, didn't appeal to her any more than the rigid rows.

Once, she might have stubbornly insisted that she loved the choking foliage—to be different, to be special, to have an idea no one else had had before, like all her friends. They all had ideas, about what clothes you should wear, about how women should be treated, about how traditions should be thrown away and morals tossed to the wind. They were a generation full of ideas, and Adele was glad to be a member.

But not anymore.

She was not one of them.

Now she saw the beauty—the true beauty—was destroyed by these noxious weeds. Choked out before it reached the sunlight. Troy had his way of dealing with the invaders; Adele didn't know what her way was yet. However, she was ready to discover it.

"We should clear out these weeds," Judy said.

"Mm," Adele replied, neither confirming or denying this statement. "No," she said. "Not now. It must be beautiful."

"If the weeds are gone, it will be beautiful," Judy said.

"No," Adele murmured. A wave of sadness washed over her. "The scars remain until you cover them ... or until they fade in time. But we should be able to cover the scars as soon as the ugly comes off."

"I guess," said Judy, brow wrinkled in confusion.

*She's too young to see the scars, or rather to know what they are,* Adele thought. *Someday, she will know, too.* "But where can we find some flowers?" she mumbled.

"You have pretty flowers," Judy reminded her.

Adele laughed. "My seedlings, yes. But those aren't meant to be put outside, Judy." They were stored in the garage which was a makeshift greenhouse since their evacuation from London. Thankfully, as of yet, Holt hadn't knocked them off the table.

"Don't flowers grow outside?" Judy asked.

"Normally," Adele said, "but not these flowers. The seedlings that I saved from our shop were for growing indoors. That's why they're in the garage."

"Oh." Judy blinked. "It's getting pretty warm. Perhaps we could put them outside, anyway?"

Adele took a deep breath. "But if there's a storm they'll be ruined."

"But maybe there won't be a storm." Judy plainly wanted to do some gardening—like mother, like daughter.

Adele ran a hand over her face, thinking hard. "Maybe there won't be. I would hate to let them die, but with careful tending ... they just might make it."

"So we can plant them?" Judy asked, excitement growing in her face.

Adele smiled and nodded. "Yes, darling. We can."

Mother took a break from her house-cleansing at this point, allowing Adele to pass Camilla off for a bit so they could really work. After pulling the seedlings in their crates out of the garage and setting them beside the thick patch of weeds, Adele and Judy examined the briars worriedly.

"We'd better start weeding," Adele said.

"We?" Judy asked, brow furrowed. She turned her face up to her mother curiously.

Adele smiled grimly. Of course Judy didn't think she was capable of work, having spent most of her life with the old Adele, but that didn't make it hurt any less. "Your father taught you well. But yes, 'we.' I can weed."

"You can?"

"Yes."

Adele hesitated another moment, then kicked off her shoes and dropped to her knees. She began ripping out the weeds almost energetically. However, she soon stopped and turned to her daughter.

"What are you standing there for? Usually you're a lot more diligent than I am!"

Judy knelt next to her mother but continued gawking at her.

"What's wrong?"

"This is work."

"I know."

"You'll get dirty."

Adele laughed merrily. "Actually, Judy, I know all about dirt. I grew up in the country. Did you know that?"

Judy shook her head.

"It's true."

"Did you like it?"

Adele cocked her head. She wasn't sure how to explain it. She'd loved her home until it wasn't much of a home anymore, then she'd hated it. But she wasn't sure how to explain that to Judy. "It was a lovely place, but I didn't care for it after my father and brothers were lost."

"Lost?"

She swallowed. "In the war."

"The one when you were little?"

"Yes. The one when I was little. It was ... it was heartbreaking for me, Judy. I never loved someone as I loved my father and my brothers, especially my brother Kenny, though they were much older than me."

"Not even Daddy?" Judy asked.

Adele smiled wistfully. "Once, Judy, a long time ago, I loved your father. But it wasn't real; it didn't last. And now ... oh, I don't know. Now it's different."

"Oh," Judy whispered. "Maybe someday you can love him again. Like how you loved me again."

Adele sat back on her heels and turned to face her daughter. "Judy, I always loved you. Since the moment you were born. I didn't know it or act on it for the longest time, though. So perhaps I didn't love you, in the action sense. But I did genuinely care about what happened to you, and I did think you were simply wonderful."

Judy sighed. "I guess that's true. I never thought you didn't care. I just thought you weren't ever going to like me that much."

"I'm sorry, Judy," Adele murmured, placing her hand over Judy's for a moment before removing it. "It's going to be better from now on. You'll see! Better for your father and me, too."

"It already is," said Judy.

# Chapter Seven

When they finished pulling the weeds, Adele and Judy painstakingly began planting the seedlings.

It was long, slow work, but Judy was a natural. Adele was actually quite proud of her. She wondered if working on this garden could be something they did together. Something that would let them talk and get to know each other—and become good friends.

Adele hoped so. Otherwise, she and Judy didn't share a lot of interests. That she knew of, at any rate.

"We don't want them in rows," Adele said. "We want them to grow all over the place. After we get the seedlings planted, we'll scatter seeds and plant bulbs everywhere. Just wherever we can find enough space for roots to grow. It'll be prettiest that way."

"And messiest." Judy wrinkled her nose like a disapproving bunny.

Adele chuckled. "Your father had his way with the vegetable portion of this garden, so I will have my way with this half."

Judy nodded. "I guess Daddy won't mind too much. At least, I don't think so."

"On this small part of my life, your father has no input," Adele said. "I've always taken care of the frills. He won't care."

Her daughter didn't reply; she simply patted gently about the roots of the seedling she was currently installing into the ground. Adele smiled. Judy was so serious and focused.

Silence stretched out before them, and Adele felt compelled to break it but wasn't sure how. What could they talk about? Something that would interest them both.

"What ... what's your favorite type of flower?"

Judy paused for a minute and cocked her head. "Cherry blossoms—and pansies. What about yours?"

"Hmm. I think roses. That's rather cliché, but there it is." She liked originality, but sometimes it was impossible. Besides, Troy always bought her roses, so it made her life easier for them to be her favorite.

"What's cliché?"

"Er, it means lots of other people like roses. They're a popular flower."

"Oh." Judy picked up a new seedling and prepared a

place for it. "But why does it matter if it's popular?"

Adele blinked. "I suppose it doesn't matter at all." She laughed. "You're right, Judy. I shouldn't change my tastes because they're like everyone else's. There's nothing wrong with being unoriginal if you're you."

Judy nodded. They worked on in silence while Adele tried to think of another conversational subject.

"Judy?"

"Yes, Mother."

"Would you like a cat?"

Judy considered this in silence for a bit as she worked. "No. I don't think so."

Adele was surprised at that. She'd thought her suggestion would be met with excitement. "But you always wanted one when you were younger."

"Yes, but Holt would eat it, and anyway, we won't be here long. After the war is over, we'll be back in France, and so I'd rather get a French cat later on."

Adele didn't know what to say to that. She sure didn't want to correct Judy's belief that animals had specific nationalities assigned to them; it was too much fun. So she let it go.

"All right, then. We'll get a cat later, when we're back in France." Though the way things were going now, that might be years away. Adele sighed. "I hate this war, Judy."

Her daughter's face scrunched up. "Daddy says all wars are horrible."

"They are. We shouldn't be in this one. The world should be tired of wars, and yet it isn't, and they rage on." Adele shook her head. Her chest was tight, but she pushed through. "Judy, war is ... war is hell. Don't you ever get caught up in the supposed glory of it, all right? It's hell. Tears apart families, makes people do things they never would have in any other circumstances ..."

Her voice trailed off. She didn't know how to describe it. Hopefully Judy wouldn't have to grow up without her father. Hopefully no one close to them would be taken this time.

But there were no certainties in war. Each man, woman, and child was at its mercy. And this war scared her. Though she tried to deny it, Germany had the potential to take all of Europe to dark places.

"Was the other war like this one?" Judy asked.

Adele had to sit still for a moment, close her eyes, and regulate her breathing. "It was different but the same. That doesn't make sense, but ... it had the same characteristics of every war, I suppose. Destruction, lost lives, emptiness. This one started for different reasons."

"What was the one when you were little about?"

"I ... I don't know." She'd heard explanations and read newspapers and lived through it, but still she didn't quite understand. It seemed senseless. Empty politics causing brutality beyond belief.

Adele wasn't exactly a pacifist, and she believed that the Allies must take the Axis down now. But she did hate that it must happen. It was a paradox; the cause she wanted and believed in was only going to cause more death and violence.

It was complicated. More than she could explain to

Judy. Thankfully, her daughter seemed done with questions for the time being.

Adele was glad. Once again, she had no answers.

Judy thoroughly enjoyed every moment of the time in the garden with her mother. They finished planting the seedlings by late afternoon then stood up, dusted the dirt off their hands and knees, and stepped through the kitchen door. Granny was starting dinner while Aunt Lola sat in the corner, cradling Camilla.

"What time is it?" Mother asked as she set their shoes inside the door on a mat.

Granny and Lola simultaneously turned to the two gardeners and gasped.

"Why, you're all dirty!" Granny exclaimed.

"I know. We both need a bath, don't we, Judy?"

Judy nodded. Indeed, she did. She felt dirty, but in a good way that meant she'd worked hard. She liked it—but was very ready to get cleaned up!

"But you hate dirt," Granny said.

Judy supposed her grandmother was as surprised as she had been. It took a bit of getting used to, but it appeared that Mother did love gardening.

"I do," Mother agreed, "but I love flowers more."

"*Flowers*?" Granny and Lola exclaimed.

"Yes. We planted some while you were busy cleaning. In fact, we planted all my seedlings from the shop, and we'll plant more later if we can find some seeds."

"You planted flowers?" Granny asked, voice raising.

Mother's chin lifted, but her hand trembled in Judy's. "Yes."

"Adele, how could you be so selfish? Are you really so wrapped up in your own world as that? With the world suffering as it is, you decided to plant a garden of useless blooms?"

"The garden is important."

"Important? How could a simple flower garden be important? Adele Collier, you are truly hopeless."

Judy winced, glancing between her mother and grandmother. *I wish they'd stop fighting, just for a bit …*

Mother's eyes narrowed. "I'm not a Collier anymore. I'm a Kee," she whispered.

Granny scoffed. "What difference does that make?"

"A great deal. The fact that I chose to marry and move into a new household is emphasized by the name-change. I am thirty-one years old, have two children, and am the mistress of this house. Please give me a little respect and human decency." With that, Mother turned and quietly left the room.

Judy stared after her until she felt a gentle hand on her shoulder and looked up. Aunt Lola smiled down at her.

"Let's get you cleaned up, dear."

"Okay." Judy followed her aunt out of the room to the bathroom. Aunt Lola helped her draw a bubble bath, then sat on the floor with her back against the side of the tub to chat while Judy got cleaned up.

Judy didn't want anyone seeing her without her clothes on now that she was practically grownup. Aunt Lola was pretty understanding but said she wanted to talk a bit about Granny and Mother.

In many ways, Judy was glad. She didn't quite understand why they had to fight, or why they had fought, and Aunt Lola would probably be able to explain.

"I think the main reason is that they're scared, baby," Aunt Lola said.

Judy paused, soap clutched in her hand, and wrinkled her nose. "Scared of what? Aren't we safe here in the country?"

"Yes … we're safe physically. But with your daddy off to war … anything could happen. And they both know it. Both of them lost important people in the last war, remember? So did I, and so did your father. It's scary for us all."

"Oh."

"Sometimes when people are frightened or anxious, they'll take it out on others. It's not right, but if we can understand, maybe we can help them."

Judy nodded slowly and sponged a bit more dirt off her knees. "How can I help Mother and Granny?"

She heard Aunt Lola take a deep breath. "Well"—Her voice came slowly as she worked through her thoughts—"the main way is to be as kind as you can be. Talk to them when you can, and don't be afraid to bring up your father. If you want to talk about him and they don't, that's okay. You can talk to me or to God. How's that?"

"Good."

"And pray for them as well as your father. Prayer helps more than you know. God always listens, and He helps us. Sometimes you can't see the way He's helping right off, but He is."

"Right." Her father had told her that. "Daddy says he might not come back from the war, but that doesn't mean God doesn't love us. But how is that?"

"It's hard to explain, really." Aunt Lola sighed. "But God doesn't … He doesn't punish us by taking away people, okay? That's one thing to remember. I thought for years … but no. His love is hard to see when bad things happen, but the bad things are a result of the Fall of Man—you know about that, don't you, baby?"

Judy shrugged. "I think so. Adam and Eve?"

"Right. Since then, it hasn't been perfect, and sometimes bad things happen even to good people. It's difficult, but it doesn't mean God doesn't love us. He knows everything that happens to us—and no one can be killed, not even by the war, without His permission."

"But … He wouldn't give permission for Daddy to die, would He?" Judy's voice trembled, and she found that her hands were shaking, too. She dropped them into the hot water.

"I don't know, Judy. None of us know. But I do know that no matter what happens, He will love us and take care of us. No matter what happens, He is good. Okay?"

"Okay." Judy didn't know how she could live without her father, but at least it was comforting to know that

God was there, and He did hear her prayers, and He did care for her. "I'm ready to get out now."

Aunt Lola stood and ducked out of the room. "Call me in when you're dressed, all right, baby? We'll have to clean out the bathtub."

"Okay!" Judy called after her.

*Flowers In Her Heart*

# Chapter Eight

Adele was settling in with a book when she heard a light rap at the door of her bedroom.

"Can I come in?" It was Lola's voice, gentle but peppy as always.

"No," Adele replied. "I ... I need some time."

There was a moment of silence before Lola spoke again. "Please? Adele, I know you and Mrs. Collier are upset about Troy being gone—I'm upset, too. But you can't fly at each other because you're tense. We have to work together. Women can get terribly catty if they're kept in small space. But we can't."

Adele didn't know how to respond to that. She agreed that the reason this fight had gotten so ridiculous so fast was because they were stressed, but that didn't change the fact that her mother simply enjoyed picking at her.

Mother was impossible. Absolutely impossible.

But perhaps she'd better hear Lola out. She stood, crossed the room, and opened the door.

"I'm not upset about Troy. I don't care for him enough to be upset over his going, unlike my mother, who loves him more than she loves her wayward hellion of a daughter."

Lola crossed her arms over her chest, blue eyes snapping in that familiar way. Adele prepared herself for a verbal battle.

"Your mother loves you half to death! She just doesn't know how to show approval of you without showing approval of your seeming lack of any sort of faith. And of course she loves Troy. She sees him as your savior from a life of sin, whether or not that is correct. And, as far as you not loving Troy, that's your opinion, but it's not mine." She jerked her chin, obviously unconvinced that anyone could not be in love with her big brother.

Adele gritted her teeth. "I don't love Troy. At least, I don't love him the way I used to."

"You're not in love with him, you mean?"

"No." Adele sighed and stepped aside to let Lola in. She'd rather have this conversation be a bit more private, even if the upstairs portion of the house was empty at the moment. "It's not the same as it used to be."

"What's changed?" Lola asked.

102

Adele adjusted the tie of her fuzzy pink bathrobe. "I don't know. I suppose time passed." All things passed away in time, and love was one of those things. It was a sad and solemn truth, but a truth nonetheless.

"Time didn't change anything for Dave and me," Lola said, shrugging her shoulders slightly.

Adele made a flipping gesture with her hand. "Dave and you have been married all these years. Troy and I are just starting over after a long separation which I spent hating him."

Lola smiled slightly. "Love is a choice, Adele."

"I tire of people saying it's a choice when I know I can't control whom I fall in love with, and I don't think I want to, either!" Adele said, flopping onto the bed. "I love or I don't. That's all there is to it."

Her sister-in-law took a seat on the edge of the bed, expression pensive. "I'm not saying that falling in love is a choice, exactly, though I don't think it's the all-powerful feeling most seem to think it is ... but real love, the kind of love you want with your husband, is a choice."

"But I don't want love like that. My parents had it, and I saw nothing passionate about their marriage." In fact, Colonel and Mrs. Collier had seemed to care little for each other except for day-to-day things. And Mother had soured her for any type of old-fashioned matrimonial bliss.

"What do you call passion and how is it different from love?" Lola asked. Her eyes were too searching, and Adele squirmed under them.

"I don't have an exact definition. It's something you feel, not something you explain," Adele said, standing and moving about the room, straightening this and running her hand over that.

"It's fear, desire, and excitement," Lola said. "Love, the emotion, takes time, Adele. You can't expect it to happen all at once—not if it's real. However, love, the action, is something you choose to do. Now, I don't know how you can go about that without God in your life ... but you can try, I suppose."

Adele shook her head. "I'm not a Christian anymore. Troy is, and he tells me Judy is, though, thank goodness, she doesn't go around spouting it."

"It's private to her, like so many other things," Lola said, picking up a small, framed picture of Judy that rested on Troy's nightstand. The second, larger picture of Adele was gone—it was with Troy, as always.

She smiled weakly. "Private to her and Troy, you mean. She shares everything with him. He is her world. I have no place in that world."

"She spent hours with you this afternoon, and she was practically glowing when I drew her bath. She loves you; she's just cautious. She wants you to be happy."

"I've been told again and again that trust takes time to build." Time and hard work, and Adele generally disliked both.

Lola smiled. "It does indeed. All your problems will take patience to solve. In the meantime, love your daughters—and Troy, when you get the chance—and spend some time with your mother ... and plant those flowers. Someday you'll do more, but one step at a time is a lot better than ten backward."

"I suppose." But Adele didn't feel as if she'd taken a step forward in years. Everything was so difficult. Even the simplest things were like dragging her body over cut glass.

"I *know* you've changed a lot. I wish I understood you a little better—we're sisters, after all, aren't we?—but I do know that I like you a lot more now than I did when we first met."

Adele chuckled. "Was your first impression unpleasant?"

"Er, not exactly." Lola shrugged. "I liked you, but when you left Troy, let's just say I wasn't feeling exactly friendly. I wanted to kill you, I think; though he had many faults, he didn't deserve your cruelty."

"You'll be surprised to hear that I agree with you. I don't ... I don't feel worthy of his forgiveness or his acceptance." Adele wrapped her arms around herself and stared out the window. "He showed me a lot of grace. I wasn't expecting that."

She honestly still didn't understand Troy inviting her into his life again. If a man rejected her so cruelly, Adele would never have had anything to do with him again. Yet Troy had welcomed her back with open arms, even though he knew she wasn't much changed. A bit, yes, but she was still the same Adele.

Broken. Stubborn. Lost.

It made sense that he believed Judy needed a mother and therefore was willing to overlook some of Adele's faults. However, he could have found another woman to fill that spot. It didn't have to be her.

Adele was replaceable. She felt so every day. There was nothing about her that qualified for or deserved motherhood—or Troy, for that matter.

She glanced at Lola, a woman who did indeed deserve children—but hadn't delivered any. How strange this world was!

"Do you ever wonder why everything is as it is?" Adele asked. "Why I had Judy and Camilla so easily when I didn't want children, and you—" She stopped herself and winced. That was a bit too personal, even for sisters-in-law.

Thankfully, Lola's only reaction was a slight nod of her head. "I don't understand it, either. God plays His cards close to His chest sometimes. But I do know it'll make sense someday—and that's the important thing."

"Yes, well." Adele sighed. "I always wonder about my brother, Kenny. We were very close. He could have made a difference in my life. He was a dreamer, and he believed in me. I think if he had lived, I would have been much happier, and a lot of things that happened to me … just wouldn't have."

"But he died?"

"Yes." Adele swallowed. "I think he was the only person I really cared about, and after he was gone, it felt like God had forgotten me."

Lola came to stand behind her and put a hand on her shoulder. "What about your parents?"

Adele laughed, a short, empty guffaw. "My father

and I were never very close—I was his sweet little girl, and I loved him in a way, but he didn't care much for me. His favorite child was Louis, without a doubt, and I was a decoration. And of course my mother and I never got along."

Lola raised her eyebrows. "Even then?"

Adele shook her head. "She's always hated me, even when I was small. Oftentimes she would yell at me for no reason, when I was too young to understand why. After Kenny died, she said I didn't care about anyone but myself and cut me off. I hated her then."

"Really? That's insane! How could she treat you like that?" Lola's brow furrowed. "A mother should protect—never destroy. I can't imagine such behavior. Why would she have acted like that?"

Feeling oddly vindicated, Adele shrugged. "I don't know. You've seen how she treats me even now. It's always been like that."

"I assumed ..." Lola's voice trailed off.

"Assumed I started it?" Adele suggested. "I suppose it would look like that. I know all my actions haven't been because of her, and I can't blame Mother for everything. But I feel that I might be able to move on a little better if she hadn't treated me so badly when I was a child."

"I can see that! I'm sure she regrets it, though that doesn't change what happened." Lola frowned. "I don't understand it. Are you sure you're remembering that right?"

Adele nodded. "I believe so. I don't remember

everything very clearly, but I do know that she lashed out at me after my father and brothers died for no reason that I could understand."

"Hmm. I can imagine she was overwhelmed by grief, but did she never apologize?"

Adele shook her head. "Never once. It only grew worse. She rarely mentions my father and brothers now, though. When she does, it's with reverence as far as my father and Louis are concerned—and disapproval for Kenny."

"Did she treat Kenny the same way she treats you?"

"Yes. My father did, too."

Lola sighed. "That is a mess."

"My family always was rather horrid to each other," Adele admitted. They'd torn each other apart, and she was starting to learn that that wasn't what a family was supposed to do. "I wish I could say that my father and brothers were perfect, but in truth, my father was often as cruel as my mother to Kenny."

"I'm sorry. Children shouldn't have to go through that." Lola pulled Adele into a hug.

Adele drew back momentarily. "Yes, well. It's just my life." She didn't feel comfortable receiving such open, honest sympathy from Lola. She didn't believe her mother was the only one at fault though she'd rather shift the blame. A lot of Adele's messy life was caused by *Adele* as indicated by her possession of said life.

"It shouldn't be."

"But it is. There are a lot of things about your life that *shouldn't be*, either. Like losing your parents. But that doesn't change the fact that ... it's our life." Adele wrapped her arms around herself. "Mother always says I'm selfish. That's what she accuses me of most often, actually—that I'm heartless, that I don't care about others. Well, I do. Sometimes I'm not great at showing it, but I do care. And I'm sorry that so many people have to live in this crazy, messed up world."

Lola nodded slowly. "That makes sense, I suppose. I don't think you're completely selfish. Naturally, I suppose, you are, but ... nobody's perfect. You have the ability to live for others in you, just like everyone else. It's a fight you have to engage in."

Adele stood still by the window, her hand on the sill, and thought about this. "You're right, I suppose. It's a fight. I always feel like I'm losing it."

"You're not! I ... I suppose you wouldn't hear me if I told you about God, but He ... I'll leave that. It's not my place. But if you ever want to talk solutions instead of problems, look it up in the Bible." Lola grinned. "I think the answers would surprise you. I'll be praying for you."

Old Adele would say, "Don't bother." New Adele simply said, "Thank you." After Lola left, she sat on the edge of her bed and thought about forgiveness and selflessness and what it meant to be a good person.

The definition was hard to pin down, but she was curious. She wondered what Lola meant by solutions and what the Bible could possibly have to offer her.

Not much, she supposed. God just wasn't for Adele. He didn't care about her anyway.

# Chapter Nine

Judy sat back on her heels and surveyed the assortment of colorful blossoms around her. At her side, her mother knelt plucking the many little weeds that sprung up about the roots and threatened to overwhelm their flowers.

How dare they! Judy scowled. "Why did the weeds grow back? I thought we got them all."

Mother leaned back and glanced around the garden. "I don't know. I suppose we didn't."

"Oh, nonsense. Seeds probably blew in," Granny said from where she sat on the old wooden bench, Camilla on her lap.

That made sense. Judy knew very well that even if

one was very careful—and they had been very careful— sometimes nasty things got into one's good things.

Mother just shrugged and went back to her picking without another word. For a long time, no one said anything, but it was a nice, beautiful kind of silence. There were birds singing and a breeze rustling the trees. Judy liked country silence. It was lovely.

"I'm going to leave Camilla in her bassinet and help Lola with lunch," Granny said at last, standing.

Judy watched her go and allowed the world to lapse into quiet again for a bit. But she did have something she wanted to talk about. Her mother's friendliness combined with the hard work had given her courage, and she wanted to try telling Mother about something very important.

Even if she was ignored or laughed at.

"Mother?"

"What, Judy?"

"I've been thinking about something and ... would you be angry if I talked about it?"

Mother set a handful of weeds down and sat back on her heels. There was an odd look on her face, like she was about to taste something unpleasant and knew it, but she nodded anyway. "Of course not. You can tell me anything."

"You know Daddy?" Judy winced as soon as the words were past her lips. What a stupid question! Now her mother would laugh. She felt her ears grow warm.

But Mother barely had a twinkle in her eyes as she replied. "He's an acquaintance of mine, yes."

"He's a Christian," Judy said. There was more to it than that, she supposed, but that was the bare bones idea.

"I know."

She took a deep breath. Here came the real confession. "I ... I am, too."

"That's what your father said."

Her chest clamped. So Mother knew, and she hadn't said word? That hurt. Though Judy supposed her mother just didn't care. Still, it was important.

For a while, she worked in silence, not able to meet her mother's eyes, then a question came to her that she hadn't considered before. She turned to face her. "Am I in trouble?"

Mother raised her eyebrows. "Why would you be in trouble for being a Christian?"

"Because you always said that it was a lot of nonsense ..." Judy's voice trailed off as her eyes dropped to hands she now clutched in her lap. "I don't want you to think I believe in fairytales anymore, Mother. I believe in Jesus, my Savior."

Mother offered a bit of a smile, but it wasn't real. Not really. "I know, Judy. I understand, and I believe God is real for you and ... and other good people, but He can't be for me." She squeezed Judy's shoulder then let her hand drop to her side. "Let's keep working."

"Could I ... could I tell you about Him?" Judy bit her lip as she waited. If only her mother would let her say it, perhaps she could be persuaded.

Mother sighed. "All right, Judy. Go ahead. Tell me

about it." Even as she spoke, she knelt down to begin work again, so Judy didn't feel that she had her mother's full attention. Still, permission to speak was something.

Judy took a deep breath. "It says in the Bible that if you aren't perfect, you don't go to Heaven. And if you don't go to Heaven, there's no other place for you to go but ... but Hell." Judy shuddered at the word.

"Mm."

She swallowed. "Nobody's perfect."

Mother's eyes flickered up to Judy and softened slightly. "You are, baby."

"No, I'm not. I sin all the time. And even if I'm not doing wrong things, I'm thinking wrong thoughts and feeling wrong emotions and ... it's just not perfect at all."

"I still think you're perfect. Or you will be. Little girls make mistakes; everyone makes mistakes."

"Exactly!" Judy relaxed her muscles at the confirmation. "But God ... God is so big and great and powerful that He just can't be around sin of any kind. I mean, He can do whatever He wants to, but we can't be around Him if we sinned. He hates sin, and sin gets in us so it's a part of us, even before we're born."

"Hmm ..."

"For a while, that was bad, because then no one could go to Heaven, and God loves everyone so much that He wants us all to come live with Him. But that couldn't happen ... so God sent His Son, Jesus, into the world to save us from our sins. He died on the cross so we can be clean. We're washed 'white as snow.'"

"I see."

Judy nodded and watched her mother's face. She couldn't tell if Mother was listening or not. "But we can't be washed clean unless we agree to be washed because God isn't going to force anyone to come to Him. He wants us to come because we love Him. So … if you want to get to Heaven, you have to 'confess with your mouth that Jesus is Lord and believe in your heart that God raised Him from the dead.'"

"And you've done that, Judy?"

"Yes." At first she'd been reluctant, but as she learned stories from her father and listened to the truth, she'd wanted to become a Christian. She believed Jesus had saved her.

Mother dumped a pile of weeds into a basket to be piled behind the fence later. "When?"

"Almost a year ago. I waited a while because I thought … I thought you might not like it. But … but I knew it was true for a long time before that. Daddy never lies, and I … I knew anyway. I've known for a long time."

"Of course you have. But you didn't tell me."

Judy dropped her eyes. She hadn't known it was her job to tell her, and she'd felt rather shy about it. After all, her mother wasn't the most enthusiastic about religious matters. "Was … was that wrong?"

"No, Judy. That wasn't wrong. It's your choice what you confide in me and what you don't. But I like to hear about everything that affects you. I know I used to say that if you could take care of it yourself, I needn't hear about it, but that's changed now. Now I want into your life. I want to hear it all. Everything that concerns you, everything that hurts you and teaches you and brings you joy. I want to know."

Judy grinned big and threw herself into her mother's arms. "I love you, Mother. I wish you could be a Christian, too. Daddy says Jesus is where joy comes from; it makes me happy for sure. But I love you anyway."

Mother's arms slipped around Judy and held her close. "I love you, too, baby."

Lola wore a light blue frock, her straw hat featuring a ribbon of a similar shade. Adele was glad she wasn't the only one who occasionally dressed impractically for gardening—it made the whole experience so delightful and was therefore unavoidable at times.

Her sister-in-law knelt among the flowers, raking her gloved hands through the soil around the tenderest seedlings. She'd officially come out to spend time with Adele and Judy and to wait for Millie—who was coming up for the weekend and had taken this Friday off to make the trip worth it. However, Adele was fast learning that Lola, like her brother, didn't like to sit still, and she'd swiftly become part of the gardening crew.

With Mother minding Camilla and Judy in somewhat of a chattering mood, the atmosphere was pleasant. Adele found herself drifting back to quiet, peaceful days wondering through gardens of rich estates in Kent. She'd visited these both when she was quite small and during her teenage years when she'd escaped her mother at garden parties, seeking the less judgmental cupid statues, trailing her fingers through the bubbling waters at the base of elegant fountains and sitting on marble benches that had rested undisturbed for hundreds of years. Those estates had been so dramatically different than her small fenced patch of fauna—yet the same sense of peace pervaded.

"'Is there a felicity in the world superior to this?'" Adele quoted softly. "'Margaret, we will walk here at least two hours.'"

Lola glanced up from the flowerbed and smiled. "*Sense & Sensibility*?"

"Yes. Though about a different type of outdoors, I rather think."

Her sister-in-law nodded. "We ought to take Judy to the seaside some time, when travel is more possible. But in the meantime, we can enjoy what we have here. Our victory flowers."

Adele laughed, though at least Lola's tone held none of the judgment her mother had frequently expressed. "I can't help myself—I have loved gardens since I was small. My Uncle Caleb had a fabulous one—well, it wasn't his, really, but his family's; however, he let me wander about it as I pleased. He taught me to ride a pony there. I used to take an armload of books to a bench there in the afternoon to be alone, but if he came upon me, he'd tell me stories about his family and his travels." She hadn't thought about him in a long time. He'd died during a time in her life when she'd been desperately unhappy—and not really known it. Self-obsessed in the way only a young woman embracing the dangers of complete freedom could be, she'd barely registered his passing, still less thought about how her Aunt Ella had held up to this sudden loss.

Of course, she'd spoken with Aunt Ella over the years from time to time, but she'd not visited. Perhaps she ought to—take the girls and make a day of it. They were only an hour or so from where she lived now.

Lola leaned back and rolled her shoulders. "I think I've loosened the soil here enough to have a positive effect, and my arms hurt now—I'm not used to this type of work. I used to spend hours out in the vineyard with Troy, but I've been such a housewife since I married. When you live in London, you forget what it is to always live three steps from a tree, from a place where you can get your shoes off and be a wild thing again."

Adele raised her eyebrows. She'd never taken Lola—always so neat, so ladylike—as someone given to wild impulses. "What does that mean to you? To be a wild thing again?"

"Oh, I don't know. To toss off my hat and gloves and stop feeling like I ought to have my life in any sort of order—to take long walks in the rain and come back with my hair a mess—and to be a child again. I haven't been a child in several decades, and I'm only twenty-nine, so you understand that's an accomplishment."

"Really?" Troy always described Millie was forever-young, the innocent that he and Harrington had fought to protect, the casualty of war he always made sure never had to be reported.

Lola stood and removed those gloves, tossing them in a wheelbarrow. "Yes, really. No matter what my dear older brother tells you. He's a fool, really, when it comes to me—and so is Harrington. Neither of them think I'm any older than sixteen, and both of them think I don't understand my own life. I'm not sure why, for Dave saw at a glance all of me, which was why I married him—to be known, to have a life in which I was in control. And because I was awfully in love with him, but I think that was part of the why." She smiled. "Of course, Dave is adorable on his own. After dragging Troy and Harington out of their constant gloom for ten years, a decade with someone who was is willing to fight for joy has been an incredible relief. When he comes back, we'll be happier still."

Adele didn't understand Lola's devotion to Dave, who by all accounts was a strange clerk with far-too-big glasses and a funny laugh, but she nodded as if she did.

"I suppose there's something of my mother in me. She was born for Paris, not for the Riviera, and I'm as much her daughter as Troy is his father's son." She winked. "I've not been to Paris in ages, though, and I don't know if I ever will be again." Her eyes darkened, but she still forced a smile. "I have memories there, though. I went with Dave about four years ago. Absolutely delighted him—he was such a tourist."

"Well." Adele cleared her throat. "When Troy and I are back at the vineyard—which we will be someday; I must believe we will be—you'll come visit, then maybe you can take me to Paris and teach Judy and I how to be natives."

Lola grinned. "I'd like that. Maybe while we're there, we'll teach Troy, too. He's hopeless, you know."

Adele had to laugh at that. That wasn't necessarily her impression of him, but then, she was a great deal less educated on what made a Frenchman than Lola. "Of course."

# Chapter Ten

Millie arrived that afternoon as promised and enjoyed fussing over Camilla and chatting with Lola and Mrs. Collier—and she finally had something interesting in her own life to chat about with Adele. Something which, of course, Adele would never let her stop talking about.

"That's adorable!" Adele exclaimed. "But, honestly, how can you work with a man for ten years and ignore him until now? He sounds sweet!"

Millie, blushing and beaming, shook her head. "Not all of us dive into relationships head first. I need more time is all. And I didn't think of him that way. He's my boss, after all—I still feel it's inappropriate for us to see each other."

"But you did agree to go out with him?" Adele pressed. She wanted her best friend to be happy, and it would seem that this Lennon Young was her best chance. Though Millie was still relatively young, Adele felt she couldn't afford to waste any more time.

"I didn't!" Millie squirmed in her seat. "It's not a date; we're getting dinner 'some time' when I'm free. I haven't set a day or a time, and it may be a while before I do."

"Oh, Millie, you didn't!" Adele cringed on the inside though she tried to keep from wincing. "Why did you turn him down? You know men; they're 90% pride and 10% stubbornness. He'll not ask you again!"

Millie burst out laughing. "Not all men are like that! And if he really wants to take me out, won't he ask again?"

"Perhaps, but what if you've missed the chance?" Adele couldn't bear the thought of missed chances. "Besides, it's not good for us to play games. You've told me that a thousand times!"

Millie frowned, apparently offended. "There's a difference between playing games and simply not being sure when my schedule will allow for a date."

"Oh, Millie, you know everything that's going to be happening in the next several months, let alone for the next few weekends!" Millie Lark was the most organized person Adele knew, and it was ridiculous for her to say she wasn't sure of her schedule. She was plainly just struggling with a case of the nerves. "Darling, what are you afraid of? He won't bite, I'm sure. If he did, he would have already. Just go out on a date!"

"Adele, I don't even know him."

"Of course you do! You've worked with the man for over ten years. What more could you know about a man before starting to date him? You're as well-prepared as you'll ever be."

Millie smiled, somewhat guiltily. "You sound like my mother."

"See? It's not just me! I'm right. You need to get out more, Millie, and this is a fantastic chance for you to reach for your dreams." Adele paused and cocked her head. "This is what you want, isn't it, Millie? To be married to a good man and all that? How can you even start if you aren't willing to have a perfectly pleasant fellow ask you out on a date?"

Millie sighed. "I suppose you're right. I just ... What if he's not as nice as he seems? I'd feel awfully guilty to turn him down."

"Why should you? A date isn't a proposal of marriage."

Her best friend cocked her head, nose screwed up in that adorable way that made her look like an annoyed pug. "I ... I suppose."

"I *know*! No man considers a woman to be bound to him after a first date. You're not committing to anything but dinner and dancing." Adele put a hand on Millie's shoulder. "You'll do fine. Why don't you talk to him Monday and try to set a date?"

"How? Isn't it his job to ask next?"

Adele moaned under her breath. The poor innocent

didn't know a thing! Oh, well. She grinned inwardly. She wouldn't mind giving her professional advice. "Dearest, you don't have to outright say, 'I'd like to go on a date with you now; how about this weekend?' No, that's crass, and his poor pride would be offended. Men want to take the lead, and I say let them."

"Then what—?"

"Hint. Let him know it'd be welcome! You're a woman, Millie, if you remember. You were born to do it."

Millie crossed her arms over her chest at that, her posture defensive.

"Oh, come on!" Adele squeezed her shoulder. "You can do it."

"Sounds dishonest."

"No, it's not!"

"Okay, sounds *flirtatious*." Millie said it like a dirty word.

Adele rolled her eyes. "Do you expect to never be flirtatious with your husband? Because I don't know about you, but I think that's rather to be expected." She winked.

Millie glared. "We're not married, and in all likelihood we never *will* be married, and it would be highly inappropriate. He's my superior, Adele!"

"At work! Not outside of it." Not that Adele thought the workplace was necessarily the most unlikely place to catch a man—she'd got Troy's attention while on her most professional behavior, after all, hadn't she?

"I don't see him outside of work."

Adele flopped back on the bed. "*Millie*!" She said her name like a dirty word—there, now Millie would know how she felt half the time. "I feel like strangling you. How can you be like this and have any fun? Is that what God wants? Because all the Christians I know are intolerable bores. This is ridiculous."

Millie laughed and shrugged her shoulders unconsciously. "I think I'm more boring than most Christians, actually. And God commands us to be joyful—He wants us to be happy and content. But that doesn't mean—"

"Then be happy!"

"Honestly, Adele, it would just make me anxious to try whatever you want me to try. Hinting for a date? Does that sound like me to you?" Millie cocked her head and raised her eyebrows.

"Well, no." Adele stood and paced across the room, hand on her chin. "Okay, how about this." She whirled to Millie, setting her shoulders as she did every time before approaching a man. Or how she *used to*, rather.

"What are you doing?"

"Giving you an example." She strutted across the room to a dresser drawers and leaned against it, fluttering her eyelashes at a seascape hanging on the wall. "Hi, there, Lenny."

Millie burst into another bout of giggles. "I don't call him Lenny."

"I'm just giving you an example. Fill in with whatever you call him." Adele turned her gaze back to the picture. "As I was saying before we were so rudely interrupted, you are looking quite dashing today. Oh, no, I love the polka dot tie. It's"—she hesitated as if searching for the perfect word—"*stunning*."

At this point, Millie had grabbed a pillow to smother her laughter—part embarrassment on her best friend's behalf, part actual amusement, Adele guessed—but she ignored her.

"Actually, I saw that there's a sale on polka dot ties going on this weekend. Oh, yes, you know the place—it's on the other side of town. Oh, yes, some wonderful ones. Purple and pink and crimson. You'd love them!"

"*Adele!*" Millie exclaimed, apparently offended on her not-boyfriend's behalf.

"As I was saying," Adele repeated slowly, "I'm thinking about running to that end of town this weekend. I've nothing better to do ..." She paused meaningfully, running her fingers along the top of the dresser. Then she looked up quickly at the painting and smiled brilliantly. "Oh, Lenny! I would love to go pick out polka dot ties with you! It is all I dream of. You, me, polka dot ties ..."

She glanced over her shoulder and said in a stage whisper, "What he doesn't know is I'm dreaming of burning *all* his ties and buying him new ones. A woman's got to stake her claim—and she *cannot* let her man go about dressed like that!"

"Adele, stop!"

Shaking her head, she returned to the bed and slipped under the covers. "It's that easy, sweetheart. If he's worth it, he'll ask again, especially if you weren't too negative last time. Which you never are—negative, I mean."

"I could never talk to a man like that. Compliment him on his ... on his tie or ... or anything." Millie lay on her side now, propped up on her elbow. "You've had lots of practice—and you didn't have to try for Troy."

Adele shrugged. It was true; Troy had asked her out with basically no encouragement. She was glad of that. It would've felt like cheating to win him through flattery and flirtation.

Though she supposed his original attraction had been appearance-based. But oh well. That was life. She knew their relationship had been messy—still was messy. However, she was glad he hadn't been another conquest whom she'd happened to fall for.

They were silent for a moment before Millie spoke up again. "I think I discouraged him at first because I was embarrassed and surprised—and a little scared. I hadn't thought about it before, really, though he is ... he's pleasant."

"Is he handsome?"

Millie didn't answer for a long time then she whispered, "Very."

Adele grinned. "Doesn't matter but it helps."

"Right. He's always been professional and kind, and he never talks down to me like some of the people at the office do. He knows I've worked hard for my job, because he's seen me do it and has done the same." Millie took off her glasses and began polishing them with the corner of the sheet. "He's a fine man."

"Good. I wouldn't want anything less for you."

"Thank you, Adele. I think you ought to know you've already got a fine man." Millie playfully nudged her arm, smiling. "Right?"

"Right, right." She didn't need it rubbed in. She knew she had a very fine man—and that she was miserably unworthy of his love.

Always unworthy. Always unwanted. Demon child.

Adele flopped onto her back. "Come on. Let's grab a couple hours of sleep. I know you'll want to get up early tomorrow and go to church with the others."

"Mm." Millie set her glasses on the bedside table. "See you tomorrow then."

"Right." Adele turned off the lights and pulled the covers up to her chin even though it wasn't remotely chilly. "Night, Millie."

"Night, Adele."

There were roughly thirty seconds of silence in which Adele sorted through her thoughts before she had to speak again.

"Millie?"

A sigh. "Are you thirteen? *Sleep*, darling—it's important."

"Oh, shut up, Miss Can't Talk To Her Crush."

"He's not my—"

"Shh, I had a thought."

"Heaven be praised."

Adele laughed. "It's just eleven, Millie. You'll survive."

"Your mother will want us up at seven." After she

said the words, she giggled, rolling over to smother them into the pillow. "Oh, my gosh, I can't believe I said that."

"We are kids, aren't we?" Adele grinned into the dark. "But seriously, Millie. What are demons?"

The silence was quite long after that question.

"Please let's not talk about this in the dark."

Adele sat up and switched on the light. "Okay, it's light."

Millie shoved herself up to a sitting position and grabbed her glasses. "Where did that come from?"

"Are you going to answer the question?"

Her best friend sighed. "Okay. Let me think. The Bible talks about them pretty matter-of-factly but doesn't give a lot of history. Basically, though, they're some sort of spiritual beings that oppose God, that seek to deceive humans, and that, yes, can possess humans if they are not under the authority of God."

Adele drew her knees up to her chest and nodded. "What else?"

"Not a lot. God doesn't share a lot about them—I think because He knows that the more we know, the more involved we could potentially get. Knowledge is power—and knowledge of evil things can be ... well, evil."

Millie rubbed a hand over her face, bumping her glasses up on her nose then sliding them back down to position. "But if we have God on our side, there is nothing to fear. He will keep us safe if we abide in Him, and I know that includes safety from demons. 'In peace I will both lie down and sleep; for you alone, O Lord, make me dwell in safety.' That Psalm something or other is one of my favorites."

"Can you stop talking about sleeping, granny?"

"That wasn't what I meant." Millie smiled then grew serious again. "So does that makes sense? Evil spiritual beings who have no real power over ... over Christians?" Her face crumpled a little, and Adele knew she was thinking that her best friend wasn't a Christian. "You're not ... you know not to think too much about that kind of thing, don't you?"

Adele shook her head. "No. It's just—that was my mother's nickname for me, sort of." She chuckled wryly. "A little demon. A witch. She thought I was evil."

Millie stared at her. "I had no idea. Wh-why didn't you tell me? I'm your best friend ... and Mama would have taken you in."

"I haven't told anyone, really." Adele wrapped her arms tight around herself. Somehow that seemed to assuage the hurt a little. "It was frightening after my father and brothers died. Those years ... Meeting you kept me going. Did you know that? How desperate for someone like you I was?"

"Oh, Adele! I ... of course I didn't know, but God did. I'm glad I was there. Even if I couldn't heal the wounds, I was *there*, and maybe it doesn't matter what might have happened. But I'm so glad!"

Incredulous, Adele's lips quirked up. "I'm glad I had you, too. I think it was grounding in a way. And seeing the happy, healthy Larks helped, too."

"Oh, gosh, I wish we'd adopted you or something, right then!" Millie threw her arms around Adele and pulled her in for a giant hug. "Think how that would have changed things."

"Rather impossible given that I'm not an orphan and my mother wasn't likely to relinquish control of her only remaining child," Adele said wryly, returning the hug. "But you were the best sort of sister—a sister who truly is my best friend."

Millie pulled back. "Okay, let's talk about this for a moment. I knew Mrs. Collier has never been ... well, she's very troubled."

"Troubled!" Adele exclaimed. "Oh, that's the understatement of the year. I don't think she deserves to get off that easily."

But she just waved her hand. "Oh, Adele, think—to lose Troy, Judy, and Camilla. That's what it was. It was three beloved people. Her best friend and lover and sweetheart and other half—"

"I think you're romanticizing their relationship based on your parents." Adele tried to lighten the statement with a little chuckle, but there it was. Her father died when she was seven, and she still knew her parents' relationship had been a mess.

"Anyway, her husband and the two sons she bore. Oh, Adele, the pain and suffering! Even if she was a cold wife and a colder mother, the grief would've been terrible. She was so wrong to lash out at you—evilly wrong. You were only a child. And I am angry for you—because no child should be told they are a demon. It's simply not true."

Adele nodded. She'd been told that many times, and

it was starting to feel real. The deeper she dug, the more the idea of being somehow irreversibly evil showed up. It was a hard fight to dismiss something she'd hidden so far within her soul.

"But … I just wonder if maybe she isn't regretting it like mad and doesn't know how to end this. She *must* love you, Adele."

"Oh, Millie, you know she—"

"No, Adele. I know she *does*!" Millie put a hand on Adele's shoulder. "Listen. She must. Just a little. You should understand—look at how you've treated Judy."

Her stomach seized and she felt sick. "That's not fair."

Millie's eyes softened. "Oh, darling, it is fair! It's fair because you treated your daughter abominably—but you've changed. It hurts, but it's true; it's also in the past. Now you can move forward. But maybe your mother—"

"Or she's just evil. Some people are evil, Millie."

"I know that! But Mrs. Collier doesn't seem like one of those people. Look how lovely she is with Judy and Camilla—and she's always been kind and respectful to me and Troy. Even to Lola she's basically pleasant. She's grumpy, yes, but not a bad person. Perhaps she doesn't know how to … how to stop the pattern with you. It can be hard! Just think how hard it's been for you to learn to love Judy."

Uncomfortable with the comparison of her relationship with her mother to her relationship with Judy, Adele lay back on the pillow. "Maybe, perhaps," she mumbled under her breath. "Seven's going to come awfully quick."

Millie sighed. "Okay. Let's talk about this later, though, okay?"

Adele shrugged. She wasn't really sure she'd ever want to talk about it again, but for Millie's benefit, she said, "Of course. Some time later ..."

"Mm." Millie hesitated then spoke again. "Could I pray for you, Adele?"

"I ... I thought you were always praying for me." Millie said so often enough; 'I'm praying for you, God will help you,' and on and on.

"Yes, but I mean now. Out loud. Are you comfortable with that?"

Adele wanted to reply, "No, of course not!" But that didn't seem to be the right thing to do. She wanted to be a good best friend—and not smother Millie's hopeless dreams that Adele could become a Christian. So she nodded the affirmative.

"Okay." Millie bowed her head and closed her eyes, and Adele mimicked her after a moment. "Dear Lord," she began, "be with Adele. Be with her as she tries to learn to be a better mother and wife ... and be with Mrs. Collier. Show her the light and the truth. You know both of their hearts, so You'll know best what they need, but ... help them. Please. I know both of them have had a long, tough road to get where they are. I think it's time for some healing to happen."

Millie paused for a long moment, and Adele peeped up at her, wondering if she was done. But Millie's head was still studiously bent, so she squeezed her eyes back shut and waited.

"Lord, I don't know what to pray for. I only know that ... that there is pain and confusion and emptiness. It is there for You to cleanse, to be truth, and to fill. So just do Your job, I guess."

Adele blinked. Goodness knows one shouldn't instruct God to "do His job." That seemed rather stupid. Also, talking to Him like that seemed disrespectful.

Not that she cared, of course. But still. Millie *did* care about that sort of thing.

"I'm out of words, so I trust You to do the rest. In Jesus's name I pray, amen."

"Amen," Adele echoed, opening her eyes. "What do you mean by all that? Asking God to do His job? Is He going to smite you now?" She grinned, but honestly, there was a level of curiosity there.

Millie chuckled. "I don't think so, or He would have a long time ago."

"If you say so." Adele shrugged under the covers and turned out the light. "Good night, Millie."

Millie yawned. "Good night!"

In the dark and the silence, Adele considered Millie's prayer. It was an oddly comforting one—though she tried not to think about it too much.

*To cleanse, to be truth, and to fill. Hmm. Nonsense, I'm sure ... but what if?*

The question echoed about her mind. Outside, the wind began whirling, and rain pattered on the roof, and thinking about the possibility of the roof leaking distracted her enough to allow sleep.

# Chapter Eleven

Adele awoke the next morning, rolled out of bed, and pulled on her bathrobe, leaving Millie sleeping. It was before seven, but her clear mind and wide eyes told her she couldn't hope to sleep again that night.

After using the bathroom and getting her hair somewhat presentable, she crept down the hall and into the nursery. Camilla was awake in her cradle, her whole fist in her mouth. Adele scooped her up and kissed her forehead.

The baby felt just right in her arms—not too heavy, not too light. There was something satisfactory about it; she'd never denied that.

She carried Camilla downstairs to the kitchen and prepared a bottle. Then she sat in a chair to give it to her, speaking softly to her daughter. Camilla's wide, trusting eyes—dark as the inside of a truffle—looked up at her, unblinking.

"Adele?"

She turned to face her mother who stood in the doorway.

"I got up to feed Camilla, and she wasn't in her cradle. I was worried." Mother's voice sounded mildly shocked.

"I have her."

"I can see that."

There was a long silence. Adele spoke first, her heart oddly softened by Millie's words of the night before. "Mother, when will you trust me? I'm trying to be a good mother; I really am."

Mother sighed and took a seat at the kitchen table. "Trust is earned. It doesn't just happen."

Adele swallowed. "It's been two years since Troy and I remarried. For two years I've been faithful to one man, tended his children, and been as selfless as I know how to be. I'm trying, Mother. I'm trying with all that is within me."

Mother's expression remained the same—tired to the point of being nearly emotionless. "I know."

"But?"

Mother stared at her for a long moment before she replied. "I know you believe you can change yourself through perseverance alone, Adele, but I don't think that's a possibility. Change comes through Christ. I've ... I've been learning a lot of hard lessons about that lately, and it's true. There's nothing any of us can do on their own."

Adele moaned. "Oh, Mother."

Mother rested her elbows on the table, apparently abandoning all pretenses of ladylikeness for a minute. Her eyes were earnest. "It's true, Adele. You're not going to change without God! You'll be the same selfish, irresponsible woman you've been since you were young, and nothing is going to change that but His strength."

Adele's heart throbbed painfully. Why did her mother always have to treat her like she was evil? It wasn't true—it couldn't be. "You could at least pretend you think I'm a human being instead of some changeling child a demon left in your cradle in exchange for your real daughter." The words were harsher than she intended.

Mother blinked and drew back. "That's not what I think of you."

"You've made it perfectly clear what you think of me!" Adele rose, cradling a suddenly fussy Camilla against her shoulder and leaving the half-empty bottle on the table. "I'm a disappointment. I failed to meet your standards, and I will be punished for the rest of my life. Wouldn't it be better if I weren't your child? That would make you happy, wouldn't it? It would give you peace. You could leave this mess behind and never look back, and if you want to know the truth, I wouldn't care one bit."

Mother's chin raised another notch. "Adele, no matter how mad you drive me, I will *never* give you up. Never. Mothers don't stop caring for their children. You should know that. I lost my husband and my sons. My family died long ago. I've no one left. You are my only reason for living."

Adele dropped back into the chair. Camilla's shriek at the jolt was a welcome distraction, and she managed to soothe the baby and encourage her to take the rest of the bottle.

When at last she raised her eyes to her mother, she found her sitting in the chair across from her, hands folded in her lap, eyes downcast.

"Mother." Adele's voice trembled around the edges. "*Why*? I don't understand. Why can't you just ... be like other mothers? Why can't you ..." Her voice broke off. The lump in her throat forbid further speech. No words would penetrate without starting a rush of tears.

"Oh, Adele." Mother sighed. "I wish I could ... I wish you knew how trapped I've been. By my own bitterness, by my anger. By things I can't begin to explain to you. Only recently, when we've been here in the quiet of the country, with all the family I've got, forced to remain still and *listen* to God, to stop doing all the talking—" She paused. "Adele, I'm so sorry. I'm so terribly sorry. I didn't know what I was doing. I don't know who I was ..."

"*Oh.*" Adele pressed her free hand to her mouth in a fist, unable to unclench her fingers, her other arm tight around her child. "It ... it wasn't my fault, was it?"

138

"What wasn't your fault?"

"K-Kenny. It wasn't a punishment. Please tell me it wasn't a punishment. Because I ... I loved him too much. I wasn't good enough to be his little sister—and God ... God took him. When he was still a boy himself."

Mother didn't reply, and as the seconds ticked by, Adele realized that, though her mother was suddenly sharing more than she ever had in the past, the basic rules hadn't changed. Her father, Louis, and Kenneth didn't exist anymore. They were a relic of the past that her mother would never explore again.

"I ... I can hardly bear it, Adele. I keep thinking if I'd supported him and loved him enough, he never would have been on the battlefield—and I never would have lost him." Mother pressed her hands to her temples. "But no. It was never your fault—even, or rather especially, the things I blamed you for. You were a child."

Adele swallowed. She hadn't thought that her mother might carry a share of guilt. "I think Kenny was going no matter what we did," she said simply.

"Yes. Perhaps. Neither was Louis either of our faults. He was my little soldier—I could not stop him from following his father." Mother shifted her gaze to the comfort of the kitchen wall. "As for your father, that was inevitable. For a long time, I thought it was my fault. Thought I willed it into existence or some nonsense, and God took both my sons as a punishment."

"What?" Adele blinked. Willed it into existence? What did that mean?

"I'd thought for years that if your father was shot, I would rejoice in my heart." Mother cut her eyes to Adele for a moment then back to the wall. "He was a difficult man to live with. He ... well, never mind. A girl ought to respect her father."

A hard weight settled in Adele's stomach. "I want to know. I'm not a little girl; I think I'll be able to handle it. Truth ... truth is important, I think."

Mother nodded. "He could be difficult—especially when he was younger. Before you were born. He mellowed. But he would drink back then, and his temper was terrible. I was frightened for the boys. Once he dislocated Kenneth's shoulder. I hated him after that. Hated that he lied to the doctor about it. Then Kenneth hated him, too, of course. I wanted to be a good wife." She paused and winced. "I didn't know that I should protect my children and myself. It wasn't the way I was raised. It's not the way a lot of girls are raised even now. But I think you know that loyalty can only go so far. No one should live in fear of their husband. That's the exact opposite of how a man should make you feel."

Adele blew out a breath. "I had no idea. I ... I thought he was a good man. I loved him."

"As I said, he mellowed, and he would *never* have hurt you, Adele. Though he wasn't always gentle with me, you softened him. He said you were his flower, worthy of protection, to be fussed over and loved on." Mother shakily removed a handkerchief from her pocket and pressed it to the corners of her eyes even though they were dry. "I was so jealous, and that sounds ridiculous, but it was true."

"N-no. I think I understand that." Adele had been jealous of the extra attention Judy got from Troy, after all, hadn't she? And when she was hurting, it got worse and bit at the back of her mind, poisoning her heart against her own child.

*Oh, God. God, help me.* The words rose in her heart, and Adele could do nothing to stop them. She'd repeated the pattern her mother had set—she had done to Judy almost exactly what her mother had done to her.

"I so badly needed someone to put this all on, Adele. You were the only person at hand. I punished you for a thousand things that you didn't do. I couldn't help myself—perhaps I could have, but I didn't want to. I turned all the pain and hurt into hate; that was easier than moving on and choosing to love you."

*Oh, God, save me.*

She couldn't shake away the thought, couldn't stop the prayers. *Rescue me. I want this to end. I want to be better than this. Oh, Lord, take away my life and give me a better one.*

Tears began to slip out. "I had no idea," she whispered, voice thick. "I ..."

"It's all right." Mother nodded, a quick up and down motion of her head. Adele could tell by her tone and the brevity of her words that she was close to crying, too. "I had no idea what I was doing. The most important thing is this moment. Would it be possible for you to forgive me? Perhaps we could begin anew."

Adele squeezed her eyes shut. Forgive her mother?

141

Oh, but all of this was insanity! She must be dreaming. Yet Camilla's fussing that threatened to turn to screams if she was not tended told Adele that it was very real—and that she had better attend to reality.

Opening her eyes, she stood and moved Camilla to her shoulder, patting her back gently. "There, there, darling. It's all right. I'm here ..." She cooed on, pleasant nonsense, and thought about her mother.

Mother hadn't moved except to shift her body more toward Adele. Her hands were in her lap, clutching the handkerchief now, and her eyes were intense.

"Adele? I would appreciate an answer."

She bit her bottom lip. "I don't know what to say, Mother. I ... I want things to change. But it's hard for me to trust you. You must understand that."

"I'm not asking for trust. I can't ask for that; I know it will probably never happen. I'm simply asking for pardon. I'm sorry; you can't know how sorry I am. You're all I have left save Judy and Camilla. I don't even have friends—I don't let myself be close to people." Mother's eyes started to water at that, but she stood. "If you can't forgive me, I understand. I did something horrible, and I know I held onto blame for things you didn't do for years. I deserve it." She turned to leave the room.

"No!"

She moved to face Adele again.

"I do forgive you." The words were hard to force out, and then it was as if she couldn't stop the rush. "I'm sorry, too. I'm dreadfully, dreadfully sorry. I've been a mess, and I shouldn't have ... I'm so sorry. I've been horrid—to Judy and Troy and you. To Millie even, sometimes. Forgive me."

Her mother's jaw tightened as she struggled with her emotions. At last she got out, "There's no need for you to ask." Then Mother straightened her shoulders and glanced around the kitchen. She nodded tersely. "Well. It looks like you have everything under control. I'll dress and start breakfast. Would eggs be all right, do you think? That nice old man from down the lane gave us a fresh dozen yesterday, and we've little else for the time being."

Adele struggled with the rapidity of the change before realizing that Mother needed a moment to recover and was seizing some calm. That was understandable. Adele needed a moment to herself, too. "I normally just have toast."

"Nonsense." Mother folded her arms across her chest. "You'll have eggs. You can't start a day without a healthy meal. No wonder you always look so emaciated. I'll be back in fifteen minutes." She retreated quickly.

After Mother left, she washed the bottle and left it to dry on the windowsill. Camilla, now satiated, rested in her basket. Adele spun the makeshift mobile, a mismatched set of kitchen utensils tied to a piece of stick with a tangle of brightly-colored string. Camilla cooed and reached for it, eyes wide with fascination.

"Now, you just stay there and don't move while I check on our flowers," Adele instructed.

Camilla made no reply save to reach even harder for her toy. Adele shook the strings again and turned toward the door.

The sun was shining now after the storm of last night, and only a few clouds lingered here or there, marring the blue. However, despite it being a beautiful day, the garden was not a pleasant sight.

Adele would have been pleased by the flower petals strewn everywhere except for the fact that they weren't meant to be strewn.

These flowers, these flowers she'd worked so hard on, were precious to her, and she couldn't bear the sight of them, dead or dying, all over the back yard.

The worst thing was there was no one to blame. No one could hold back a thunderstorm—except God, and He owed her no favors. There was no point in blaming anything but the rain and the wind for this disaster.

Still, the fact remained. Adele's flowers had been cut down ruthlessly in the prime of their bloom, scattered about the yard, lying in damp, muddy tangles everywhere.

She wasn't sure if she wanted to cry or scream or hit someone. She only knew she was angry, and, for once, there was no one to direct that anger at. She couldn't even yell at herself, for there was nothing she could have done. Cover them until the storm passed? Nonsense. What would she have covered them with and how could she have known a storm was about to brew?

There was no release to be had, so Adele turned away from her garden, all the sunshine in the world blocked from her, and marched around the house.

# Chapter Twelve

Out in the open countryside, Adele made her way up a rather steep hill dotted by cows who never even raised their heads to look at her. At the crest, she found a large rock, sat down, and began to cry.

She wasn't sure why she was crying. She was just so disappointed. In herself, in the failure of her flower garden, in what she'd come to.

Adele had become her mother, and she wasn't sure how to get out. There seemed to be no avoiding it, and she was heartbroken at the prospect.

What if she wasn't able to change? Though her mother vowed that things would be different now, that wasn't necessarily true. It was very possible that their relationship would continue on as it always had before.

Painful. Hurtful. Degrading. Everything a mother and daughter's relationship shouldn't be. And that would, of course, translate to her relationships with Judy and Camilla.

What if she was incapable of doing anything right? What if she was beyond forgiveness? What if her life had been torn to shambles, too far gone, and this was only a temporary reprieve?

What if Troy died in the war? How would she go on without him? Without the man she … Yes, she'd say it. The man she wanted to spend the rest of her life with.

What if Troy did come home and they quarreled? What if he sunk into the bottle for comfort? She was vaguely aware he'd struggled with drinking in the past. It could happen again.

She trusted Troy deeply, but there was nothing about her past life that had been sure—why should he be? What if he changed, became violent, hit Judy? Anything could happen. People changed, most often for the worst, and there was nothing she could do to stop it from happening.

Helpless. She was helpless in a big, heartbreaking, ruined world. A world full of so much pain and emptiness that she could scarcely breathe as it pressed down on her.

"Evil," she whispered. "It's so evil here. It's so endlessly, wickedly, horridly evil here. And the people who live here are worse—both for the evil they cause and the evil they reflect within.

"I hate this world. I hate the people in it. And … and

I hate myself."

There. She'd said it. Hate. She hated this, and she wanted out.

*But where could I go? The only escape is death, and I ... oh, God, would I go to Hell? What is Hell?* Certainly Hell couldn't be better than this earth, but the question was, could it be worse?

*At least in Hell I wouldn't feel so guilty,* she thought. But perhaps she would. She didn't know how Hell worked. Was one still aware of the reason for the punishment or was it just endless pain with no release?

*That's what life is. Suffering. So what's the difference?*

The answer came to her in an odd way. She wasn't able to describe it, but it was there on the tip of her tongue, and she whispered it so the idea could be given life: "On earth, there is hope. Hell is where hope ends."

Hope. How stupid. She hated herself for saying it aloud, for even thinking of it. But no, it was true. It rang true in her heart.

*Hope for what? Oh, Lord, I can't hope for Heaven anymore. I don't even know You! I don't know what it is to be a Christian. I've been gone too long—no, I was never truly saved. Not really.*

Yet the idea wouldn't leave her alone. *Hope. Hope. You still have hope.* She couldn't let the thought go.

She wished she understood a little better what it meant. She thought of going to her mother and asking where her revelation came from, and why she was so determined to change now. To receive forgiveness.

What her mother told her was painful, but the truth behind it was freeing. Adele hadn't even known she'd wanted her mother's forgiveness—hadn't known the rejection still hurt. But talking about it had helped, and the feeling was strange but good.

Never would she have guessed her father was abusive, her mother felt obligated to remain with him instead of staying out of a type of love, and her brothers had been hurt by him when they were small.

But it made sense. The pieces of the puzzle started clicking together, and the sounds of their clicking were welcome. Yes, freeing was the right word. It wasn't just nonsense now; it was a life influenced by various factors, many of which were not at all her fault.

*Though some of it is my fault. No matter what my mother—or anyone else on this earth—did or said, I am responsible for my own actions. I believe in responsibility, I think. We can't go endlessly blaming others for our problems.*

So there was no freedom there. She was still bound by her actions—and by the possibility that her actions would worsen in the future.

"Oh, God, I can't hurt my girls! I don't want to. I want to be a good mother. But what if—You see how my mother snapped. That could happen to me, too. The world is so unpredictable. Troy could die, we could divorce again, one of the girls could be hurt or leave me … Too much could happen. What if—?"

All the what if's flew about her, endlessly pulling her into a cycle of fear and worry and anxiety. There was no relief. No assurance. It was so maddening, so unpredictable. If only she could be safe. If only there was some way to assure herself of the future.

She sighed when she remembered Millie's way of dealing with the insanity. God. Always God. She shook her head. That was no good.

God didn't keep bad things from happening through prayers or obedience. He was unpredictable, too. Why, she'd prayed for Kenny's life and been as good as a seven-year-old child can be expected to be ...

And still Kenny was dead. She'd lost him forever.

*Why? He was so young. So handsome and brave. And he would have made such a difference in my life. I needed him desperately, and You took him away.*

She could never forgive God for that. No, He wouldn't help her. He didn't love her. If He did, her life would have been easier. Things would have gone her way more often.

Millie was wrong. God wasn't safe. If He was anything, He was a terror-causer. She'd read the Bible, and she knew He'd done horrid things. What kind of being called plagues down on people?

Surely not a safe one. Surely not one she could count on to make her life better. No, there was no hope in that. There was no hope in anything. It was just pain, pain forever.

Adele stood then and glared up at the sky. "I wish You were just a little ... a little more *nice*. If you had half the empathy of any pleasant fellow you meet on the street, I would be a Christian. I need someone I can count on, but I can't count on You. Look at my life! What have You done to it?"

There was no answer from the sky.

"I'll tell You, then, though I'm sure You know. Kenny is dead—my beloved Kenny. You let my mother be abused by her husband for twenty-five years before You killed him. Even when You did, You left her so bitter and scarred that she hurt me for almost all of my life. You took both her sons when she needed them most. You took Millie's uncle and countless, thousands of others."

She paused to give God a chance to explain Himself, but there was no explanation. She didn't expect one in her heart. There was no excuse for that kind of destruction, if indeed He was in charge of things. Which she presumed He was.

"What about this new war, huh? What kind of madness is this? We've barely recovered from the last one, God! I know I haven't. England hasn't. France hasn't! I don't know what Germany is thinking; they had it worse than us, I've heard. And yet You still insist on another war. You take our latest generation and some of the old one, and what are the mothers and wives left with? Nobody. And we need our men, God, because You have so orchestrated to leave women defenseless in their absence.

"Why did You make us like this? Or why did You allow the world to turn us into this, if we weren't designed to be nothing but homemakers, weaker and gentler? Don't You see that, as it is, we need men in this world to stand up and lead? You're taking them all—the good ones die first. Why?

"And what of the children, God? What of the poor babies who will never know their fathers—and what of the women driven half mad to be two parents at once?

"How can we go on like this, Lord? How much can the world suffer before You end us? I'd be more likely to love You if you were to take us now—but I know You won't. Do you sit up there on Your golden throne eating bonbons and laughing at how we struggle? I hate You. I *hate* You!"

Exhausted, she dropped to her knees, cradling her head in her arms, and lay there trembling as the tears came again.

Her soft weeping had turned into sobs that cut her in half and made her teeth chatter when a pair of arms stole around her and pulled her close.

"Oh, Della, I had no idea."

"Troy!" Adele threw herself into him and held him close. "Darling, what are you doing here?"

"I'm off for a few days. I got in on the first train this morning." He pressed her close and kissed her forehead. "You weren't at the house, so I came up looking for you. Here you were, screaming at the sky. Oh, Della, why didn't you tell me?"

"T-tell you what?" She scrambled for a handkerchief then realized she was still in her dressing gown. "Oh, gosh."

How crazy the cows and God must think she was.

"Here." He pressed a slightly rumpled, suspicious-looking hankie into her hand then shrugged off his jacket and placed it around her shoulders. "It's all right. Settle down. Do you need to cry?"

"No. Not right now, anyway." The outburst had been temporary—and she was so glad to see him. She cupped his face with her hand and brought his forehead down to rest against hers. "I have something to tell you."

He raised his eyebrows. "I know, and I want to talk about it!"

"No. It's not about"—she gestured to the sky—"about all *that*. It's personal. I ... Troy, I want you to know that I love you." She let the words sink in but placed her fingers over his lips when he started to reply. "Shush. I don't need you to tell me a thing. I've not been brave enough to say it before—and I don't think I really knew for the longest time." Adele took a deep breath. "I also think you ought to have it on your mind that if you die, my heart will be broken. I believe I could live without you, but I don't want to. I don't ever want to."

"Della—"

"You don't have to reassure me or tell me I've been a good wife, and I know you love me. You can't promise to come home; it's not in your power."

"*Adele*, may I have a turn now?"

She laughed a little. "I suppose."

He placed a hand on each of her shoulders and stared into her eyes. "You've made me the happiest man in the world. Right now, with those words. I've hoped and prayed you'd be able to say it someday—and really mean it."

"I do mean it."

"I believe you; I can see it." He started to stand then sat back down; she could feel the nervous energy in him. "I—gosh. I love you, too. But I don't want to get distracted by this."

Adele thought that was a very good thing to get distracted by. She sniffled. "I suppose you want to talk about my ... my outburst."

"Right. Come sit in my lap and let's talk about it."

Adele blew her nose and wiped her eyes. "J-just how much of that did you hear?"

"I think most of it. I came in on a familiar topic—Kenny—and stayed back to hear you out." He visibly swallowed. "Then I had to come and hold you."

"I'm awfully glad you did." She leaned against his chest, tugging his jacket tight around her. Though it was mid-June and warm enough, she still felt vulnerable. *Serves me right for marching out here like a madwoman. But God knows I've some demons to exorcize—though not literal ones, I guess.*

"I am, too." He snuggled her close and dropped his head on her forehead. "But we're going to talk, okay, love? I'm so worried for you! Della, my most darling wife, you've misinterpreted quite a few things about Christianity and about God!"

Offended, Adele pushed back and met his eyes. "No, I haven't. I've read the Bible. I've gone to church, when I was young as well as a few times with Millie. I've heard all the sermons. But as I grew older, I realized that God could never be a part of my life. Why, when people don't obey Him, He sucks them into the ground!"

Yet Troy shook his head, those blue eyes that intense shade of gray that she both loved and hated. "Again, you've got God all wrong!"

Scowling, she decided to hear him out at least. "How so?"

He cocked his head. "That incident was in the Old Testament, to begin with, and an isolated one. What happened was a group incited rebellion against God. I think that an example needed to be made. They chose to rebel, and they were doing it quite thoroughly, if I remember correctly. But that was then, and this is now."

Adele shook her head. "That doesn't change anything. He's still the same God." *And He still takes lives even now, just in different ways.*

"Yes, but—"

"I just don't think it's for me. I'm not a little girl anymore. I've moved past it. I suppose I've never thought of myself as a good person, and I never will."

"But—"

Adele moaned. "I know, I know! Grace and all that. I've heard it before. Christians say that, and then they turn around and spurn me as if they aren't sinners, too. Apparently my sins are worse than theirs. But what have I done, really? Every action I've made has been out in the open, even if I wasn't proud of them all. Is that why? Because I had no shame for years, they think that Man who supposedly died for our sins only applies to them? Why? I don't understand, Troy."

Troy ran a hand over his face. "Even Christians do wrong things, Della. Christ's example was not to shun the lost. Christians should show them an example of how it should be."

Adele folded her arms over her chest. "Then I've never met a true Christian. Save you and Millie. But that's different. And anyway, you heard me. God is not nice, and I don't want anything to do with Him."

There was a long silence before Troy said, "Darling, you must know the Creation story, and you must know about the Fall of Man. I won't insult your intelligence by explaining it. But *we* let sin into the world."

"I didn't."

"Yes, darling, you did, and I did. We would have."

"I most certainly—"

"Adele." Troy placed a hand under her chin and made her look him in the eye. "You would have. Same as Adam and Eve. You wouldn't have chosen God over everything if you were offered it. You *would* have."

Adele took a deep breath. "I would have." She knew it in her heart. Though she might act as if she was a saint and say, 'I never would have bitten that apple,' she lied.

And Troy never could have let her eat it alone. Could not have chosen God over everything, same as her.

"So it is our cross to bear, Della, but it is not God's fault. Sin is what happens when we move away from Him, and now we live in a fallen world. But you know it all—darling, you tell me you've read the Bible, so of course you do. You *know* He sent His Son to save you from the world you created. You *know* He loved you enough to die for you. More than that—He loved you enough to take your punishment and your sins on

Himself.

"Oh, Della, He's not safe! Not exactly. He's not going to wash away your life—He can't take you out of this world quite yet. Not until you come to His arms in death. But He will give you everything you need to survive here. His spirit, His strength, His grace, His love.

"And darling, think of this—He's promising you eternity. Eternity is so much more than the eighty or ninety years we're given on earth. 'And God shall wipe away all tears from their eyes; and there shall be no more death, neither sorrow, nor crying, neither shall there be any more pain.' That's what Heaven is."

Adele wrung the handkerchief limp in her hands. "I could never get there."

"Oh, darling, you can!"

"No. I'm not ... not good enough."

"Della." He fake-scowled. "We're not back to that again, are we? It's not about you. This is so endlessly *not* about you. You don't have a *thing* to do with it—you could be a murderer or a figurative angel, and neither would matter. All that matters is that, here and now, you accept Jesus Christ as your Savior. That's it. He does all the work—He cleanses, He loves, He gives you what you need. From that moment on, your only job is to let Him be your Lord."

She wanted so badly to hope—but no. Troy was different. He couldn't see how desperately unworthy she was. "You don't know that He wants me."

Troy shook his head and started quoting—"'For God so loved the world that He sent His one and only Son that *whosoever* believes in Him shall not perish but have everlasting life.' 'Because if you confess with your mouth that Jesus is Lord and believe in your heart that God raised Him from the dead, you *will* be saved.' 'And it shall come to pass that all who call on the name of the Lord shall be saved.' I have more but that's what comes to mind."

Adele jerked her head up and down in a tight nod. It made sense—yet it was such a mighty commitment.

He leaned back. "But really, Della, I don't know a thing about your heart except what you've told me. So you'll know if and when you're ready. This is between you and God, not you and God and me. I want you to know that. I can't be responsible for your salvation. Only you can be. Still, I want you to know that you are wanted and treasured by God. I know you are."

Not knowing what to say, how to respond, Adele just sat still, leaning against her husband, and thought hard.

Her eyes were fixated on a daisy which waved in the wind at her feet.

The flowers in her garden which she'd so carefully tended had died ... but this little creature, all by itself up on this hill, submitted to the mercies of the wind and rain, tended by no man, had survived.

She remembered a verse about God tending the flowers. Could that be why this one had survived? Could that be why hers hadn't?

All her life, she'd done things by herself for herself. She had never truly leaned on another person; the world and everything in it was too transient to offer steady support.

She couldn't even count on herself at times. But what if there was Someone out there whom she could count on, no matter what, for the rest of her life? Was it possible that, though He couldn't offer her entire protection over her loved ones, He could offer her eternal protection and the courage to face each new day?

She wanted it. She wanted it desperately.

"What did you do with Judy when she told you she was ready?" Adele whispered.

"I prayed for her, and then she said her own."

She took a deep breath. "I'm ready."

Troy cupped her chin in his hand and tilted her face up to his. "What?"

"I'm ready."

His lips quirked up at the edge and joy filled his eyes. "Della. Darling. Are you sure?"

"As I'll ever be."

Troy wrapped his arm around her and began to pray.

# Chapter Thirteen

Judy stepped into the kitchen and froze. Her heart pounded, and her knees shook, but she propelled her feet forward nonetheless—right into her daddy's arms.

"Judy!" He swept her up and held her tight.

She buried her face in her shoulder. "No one said you were coming."

"I didn't know myself." He stroked her hair for a moment then set her down on her own two feet and took her hand. "Have you been good while I'm gone? That was a test run for me not being here, and I need a full report."

"I guess it went okay." She squeezed his hand, at a loss for words to describe the emotions pelting about her chest.

"Daddy came back this morning and surprised us. It was awful of him." Mother sat at the table with Camilla cuddled in one hand, her free hand holding an egg-laden fork. Her tone was light, but she'd been crying.

Judy looked up at Daddy. "I need to whisper something."

He bent over, and Judy cupped her hands around his ear. "Mother has been crying. How come?"

He drew back, a slight smile on his face. "Sit down and have some eggs. We'll tell you."

Why was he smiling if Mother was sad?

After she was seated, a plate of scrambled eggs placed before her, Mother and Daddy both sat at the table, looking giddy.

"Your mother's decided to become a Christian."

Judy's mouth dropped open, but she forced her lips to close. "I ... really?"

"Yes, really." Mother shifted Camilla to her shoulder and rubbed her back. "Your father met me—outside, actually—and prayed with me. I don't know everything, but I'm going to do my best to learn more about God."

How could that be true? Yet her parents both seemed serious—happy but serious.

"It helped to talk to you, Judy. Remember, you can't be in charge of me, because you're my little girl, not vice-versa, but you still did help me, even though it's not your job." Mother glanced at Daddy, and he nodded. "Your daddy wanted me to tell you, though, that this is in God's hands. He is the one who will make any changes in me. I'll do my best, but I'm not going to be anything more

160

than a baby Christian." She shrugged. "I suppose Camilla and I will both be infants together. Won't that be fun?"

Judy blinked. "I guess." At the moment, she couldn't think of much of anything. There were too many thoughts in her mind to allow a thorough perusal of any of them. Her mother a Christian? Her daddy back home, even if it were only for a day or so? She couldn't sort them all in the slightest. She ended up fixing her eyes on the top of Camilla's fluffy top and stuffing her mouth with a large bite of eggs.

"We've made the poor thing speechless," Mother mused, her hand coming up to stroke Camilla's head. "I'm sorry, Judy. I know this is a shock!"

Judy nodded. It was indeed.

Daddy and Mother and eventually the other grown-ups made breakfast a lively meal, chatting amongst themselves, joy infiltrating their circle in a beautiful way. Judy's heart was leaping, but her body didn't dare, less she ruin the delicate balance that existed in the kitchen just then.

Of community, of happiness, of family. Judy had never had a family before. Not properly. Now she did.

They finished eating, and the grown-ups cleaned the kitchen while Judy mostly watched—observing her mother, watching for any trace of dishonesty in that familiar face. Mother was everything but a liar. But how could this be?

Judy longed for her mother to be a Christian. She was old enough to know that there wasn't a lot of hope for her parents unless they both started fighting for the same thing, and she wasn't a little girl anymore, so she knew that couldn't be just her. It couldn't even be Camilla. It had to be something big.

Yet this felt too good to be true, and too sudden to have any staying-power.

"Now we have to go outside and tend to the garden," Mother said.

"It's not as bad as you think." Daddy lifted Camilla's basket; the baby had been tucked safely inside. "I'll help you clear out anything that's badly damaged, and whatever's blown in from elsewhere. After that, I think a lot of your flowers have survived. When I get home—yes, *when*; don't give me that look—we'll put together a hothouse, whether that be here or at the vineyard, but for now, you're going to have to be more practical about what you plant outside. Also, the southern-facing windows would work for potted flowers ..."

He rambled on as he walked out the back door, Judy and Mother behind him. The way Mother looked at him made Judy squirm with both delight and a degree of embarrassment that she couldn't quite explain. She only knew that, once Camilla was placed under a tree, they chose to work close to each other—and Judy made sure she could watch them.

They talked together—mostly, her mother was asking him questions about God and the Bible, and he was insisting that he would only be here for a while, so she should be seeking resources, not answers. They both called on Judy for defense of their points of view, and then they both apologized—there had been an awful lot of apologizing to Judy lately, and she grew tired of it. Daddy said she "wasn't going to spend her entire childhood as a mediator." Judy had a basic idea of what that meant, but she liked being a mediator. What a pretty word it was, after all!

Still, Daddy always would insist that he knew what was best, and he must, as a grown-up.

"What I think you should do is try to fill yourself with the Bible." Daddy tossed another armload of crushed flowers onto the growing pile. "Read it, study it, memorize it, quote it to yourself. Keep a journal and record your findings. The best way to do it would be to study it with my sister and your mother, though perhaps you might be more receptive if you were to communicate your findings with Millie. You could call each other every evening and share your thoughts—I know she would not lead you astray. Then I want you to read to Judy— remember, you may be new here, but you are her mother. That's actually what I'm most excited about."

"Me being Judy's mother?" She arched her brown eyebrows. "That's always been the case."

He scowled at her, but the expression evaporated before it had time to take root, and Judy breathed a sigh of relief. He was only joking. "I'm excited that I get to raise Judy with you and instead of in spite of you." He tossed a twig her way, nearly striking her arm, but there was a teasing glint in his eyes. "Baby, you'll listen to your mother, won't you?"

"Yes," Judy said, though she always had, even when,

sometimes, the things she said hurt.

They joked and chatted for another hour or so until the garden was clear. Then they stood together, surveying the area. Daddy slipped his arm around Mother's waist, and she leaned into him.

And Judy started crying.

Here she was, sitting in the mud, the hem of her dress stained with grass from all their efforts, tears flooding down her face.

Daddy saw her first and walked over, murmuring confused, comforting things. Mother came, too, and pulled Judy into her lap—even though Judy was far too old to be in anyone's lap, let alone her mother's—and crooned to her, her fingers tracing over Judy's legs and arms as she asked if there had been a bug bite, a thorn, anything that would make the outburst make sense.

Judy shook her head. No, it wasn't that kind of sting that had caused these tears. She didn't know why she was crying, only that she was.

"Here." Daddy pressed his handkerchief into her hand. "It's okay, Della. Let her cry as long as she needs to. There's a lot going on in our baby's life right now."

As if protesting her lack of involvement in this family-themed situation, Camilla began wailing, and Daddy fetched her while Mother stayed with Judy, crooning her name, now apparently resigned to accept the nonsensicalness of these tears.

It didn't make any sense. Judy just had tears running down her cheeks for no reason, and that was as far as her thoughts went. There were sensations, yes—of tightness in her chest, of her throat feeling full, of an ache in her stomach. Yet she wasn't sure if they were heralds of good or bad. Was she relieved or frightened?

They all went inside and got cleaned up, and once a cool rag had been passed over her hot face, a lot of the symptoms went away, and the tears stopped coming. Mother, Daddy, Camilla, and Judy all sat in the parlor together then, and Judy had to be questioned, of course. They'd been considerate at first, but they couldn't be forever. In the real world, emotions must be explained. Judy should've known that.

"It wasn't really anything," she managed, despite the fact that talking made her feel like weeping some more. "It was just that having a family is a lot more than I'm used to."

Daddy and Mother glanced at each other. Mother shrugged and concentrated on rocking Camilla while Daddy watched Judy, his face screwed up.

"I just worry about you. You must keep telling us all about these tricky feelings, even if you can't exactly explain why. It'll be so good for all of us to hear more about you. Okay?"

"I guess so."

"No." Daddy cupped a hand under her chin, and she was forced to meet his eyes—they were like hers, only she preferred them greatly to her own. Somehow, they were softer, kinder, and smarter than Judy's, with that playful twinkle she knew so well. "I know so. We will never be in any position to make promises, and to do more than 'guess,' as you so often put it, baby. However, while I breathe, I will remember you—so will all of us. You're important. Don't you dare be forgotten. Don't you dare 'guess' when you have every right to assume and declare."

Mother placed her free hand on Daddy's arm. "Do you think—?"

Daddy's eyes never left Judy's, though. "I think you say 'I guess,' even if you *know* it, because you don't want to commit to potential controversy—to cause a row, really. You don't know how the people around you will react, so you're always guessing. Hedging your bets. But you know what? That is no way to live. If you understand nothing else from me, Judy, it should be that." He blinked, and a tear slid down his cheek, and Judy was obliged to rub it off for him, as he did not let go of her. "I want you to live the rest of your life free. If I know anything about the past, it's that it wants to bind us. It binds us away from Jesus Christ—it labels us as broken failures, mortally wounded husks. But that is not what God calls us. That's something we don't have to guess at." He leaned back and turned to Mother. "I need you to remember that for me, too. Because I can't be here—"

"You'll be back." Mother's voice was damp, too. Were they all going to be messy all day long? Judy hoped not. She was beginning to develop a headache, and she felt sticky all over. "You'll be back, and we'll work through all of this. But in the meantime, yes, I will remember that."

Daddy took her hand and rose, pulling Judy into his lap, despite her weak protestations. Mother laid her head on his shoulder, the now-sleeping Camilla still cradled in her arms.

They sat like that for a long time, and some time later, Judy could explain a bit more—about Daddy leaving, about having a real family now, and about how there were so many things to trust ... so many things that weren't proven.

There still hadn't been an easy solution, but she wasn't going to let her daddy down. If he said they mustn't hold on to the hurt, she would not. Her faithfulness to him would not and could not be doubted, for she could rely on that.

Trust took time to build, but there were actions in love that she could readily perform as she waited for the beauty of certainty. Besides, Judy had learned to be the patient sort.

# Chapter Fourteen

*August 1940*

The days slipped away until, at last, August blew in, a dreary summer but a summer nonetheless. It would seem that the frequent rainy days weren't likely to end any time soon, but today, at least, the clouds had parted.

Due to the persistent rain, Adele usually read the Bible with Judy in the kitchen. However, today, the sun sparkling on dew rops had led to dragging picnic blankets up onto the hillside.

There, amongst the soft grass still scattered with an entirely new bouquet of colorful wildflowers, they laid out blankets, and Judy played with Camilla, who had now perfected rolling over. This could lead to disastrous results if they were not careful, especially on this hillside.

While Judy played, Adele read from Exodus, which she didn't like—but she was reading through it from the start now that she'd done as Troy said and read through John and a few other small books toward the end. She remembered a lot of it from her childhood, yet it was different now. If nothing else, her tastes had changed— for she did not remember the stories making sense before now.

They didn't seem as senseless and cruel as she'd thought. A new understanding rose in her that grew greater every day, and she wanted to know more.

Camilla was tired and fussing by the time Adele finished, but she quieted when Adele took her and cradled her close, kissing her rosy cheeks and toying with the increasing dark curls at the top of her head. Everyone kept saying they would fall out, but they had yet to. Adele prayed they wouldn't. Though she considered Judy to be a beautiful child, her vanity was soothed by this lovely baby who closely resembled herself in coloring, whereas Judy had inherited her looks from her aunt and paternal grandmother.

Once Camilla was settled, dozing in Adele's arms, she began to read again—Acts, because Troy said they ought to do Old and New Testament both, and Adele was determined to follow Troy's requests as if they were laws.

With, of course, a dose of grace, for she was not

perfect. She'd forgotten the struggle that forming a habit was—unless it was something bad for one, in which case it came far too easily somehow.

She had to stop every so often to scribble down something to ask about later. Usually, Adele could puzzle through things on her own, but a few details eluded both her and Judy.

"'And when they had prayed, they laid their hands on them.'" Adele cocked her head. "Do you understand that, baby?"

Judy shrugged. She'd taken to collecting wildflowers to make into a crown, and she was greatly preoccupied.

"'Laid their hands on them' sounds violent, but I don't think it is. I'll ask Aunt Lola or Aunt Millie later. Anyway, let's keep going. 'And the word of God increased; and the number of the disciples multiplied in Jerusalem greatly; and a great company of the priests were obedient to the faith.' What a time to live in! It seems every chapter has something to that effect. Though you remember I didn't much care for the last one."

Adele's soul still campaigned for her own form of justice. Millie said it was best to keep bringing such feelings before God and to others, but as of yet, that had only helped Adele minimally. Lola referred to it as 'her first struggle to trust,' and Adele wanted to struggle through and emerge a champion. Yet it was such a long process.

The chapter left off at a tricky place, causing Judy to drop her flower chain and protest. But Adele shook her head.

"Makes us more eager for tomorrow." But the real reason she had chosen not to read Chapter 7 of Acts to Judy today was because she wanted to talk it over with Millie first. During a quick skim-through, she'd realized she wasn't ready for martyrdom, and she worried about explaining it to Judy when her own faith was so weak.

Millie would probably tell her the same thing she always did: "Just do your best." Yet Adele felt the pressure, the mighty responsibility, like a weight around her shoulders. With every day that passed, she understood more—and then less again. It was exhausting, and the additional need to pass what she could on to Judy added to her feelings of incompetence.

She couldn't be enough for both herself and her daughter—yet she must be, somehow. If only Troy were here ... but he wasn't.

Lola termed those feelings of ineptitude as nothing more than that—feelings. Her sister-in-law was regaining her briefly-lost optimism, though it had never really faded at all, and as such, she'd become Adele's primary source of quick inspiration or advice. And if Lola thought Adele had only to lean on God and she could move mountains—or at least, change the way her family interacted with Christianity—then she could.

Or she must. The two were blurred sometimes. But the more blurred the lines between 'could' and 'must' got, the more Adele found herself able to handle any scenario.

As if called by Adele's thoughts of her, a light green

dress caught Adele's eyes—and there was Lola, walking up the hill with one hand clutching her straw hat. The breeze was starting to pick up, and Adele shifted Judy in her arms.

"There you are! We'd wondered if you were coming."

Lola's laugh rippled across the field like the bubbling of a brook. "I got held up at the pastor's wife's house. Those children! She has a dozen of them now, and none of them are happy, of course, with their parents in danger, all alone and in a strange place. I can't help but stay and help longer than I intended every time ..."

As she approached the small group and motioned for Judy to help her fold the blankets, she babbled on about the children and Mrs. Ichabod and how much she enjoyed helping there.

Adele stood to the side, patting Camilla's back as she was now fussing for her bottle, and watched Lola's face. *Was there anything to what Troy kept hinting about in his letters?* He seemed to believe that his sister's heart was softening toward adoption, and that *when* the war was over and *when* Dave came home—for they could not live on *if*s anymore than they could have faith in what they didn't believe—she would agree to open her home to a child or more than one child in need.

Lola carried the blankets and Judy put on her flower crown and clutched a small posy of small yellow flowers, and they proceeded back to the cottage to start dinner— and feed the increasingly grouchy Camilla.

Rain started just as they came to the garden gate, and they dashed inside. Mother greeted them, Camilla's bottle already prepared and towels folded on the chair to dab at the slight dampness that the sudden cloudburst had caused.

Adele found herself laughing.

"What is it?" Mother's eyebrows raised, though Adele could see it was curiosity, not disdain, that caused them to do so.

"We're becoming a well-oiled machine, which is funny because we've always been anything but." Adele rubbed the towel over her face—she'd learned that if she was going to be outside at all during this tempestuous weather, makeup was not an option; plus, she would run out of rouge sooner or later. "You had Camilla's bottle ready, and you knew the rain would start and we would need towels. You've set the table but left the cooking for Lola and I—and even though Lola was late getting back, and I wasn't keeping track of time at all, we aren't late."

No one else thought this observation was worth a laugh, but Lola did smile and chatter about how glad she was they were getting on well. She then told Mother all the stories she had just told Adele. That was all right— Adele had a salad to make, mostly using things from Troy's vegetable patch, and she talked softly to Judy while she worked. Judy was a master at peeling carrots and cutting tomatoes.

The telephone rang, and Adele glanced at the clock before going to pick it up. Millie liked to call right before or during dinner, because she never remembered to eat it herself and was therefore unaware of the interruption. Adele didn't mind. It made a nice routine.

They chatted for a bit then Millie told Adele that she had to "get ready."

"Get ready for what?"

There was a long silence.

"Millie!"

"Well ..."

"Camilla Faith Lark!"

"All right, I mean, it's not that important, but I agreed to go on a date with Lennon Young. Which I'm still unsure is entirely appropriate, but since I transferred out of his department last month, my excuses have seemed rather shallow. He *is* a Christian, though I only know the basics of his beliefs—"

"But that's what dating is for. You have to learn about each other, Millie!" For whatever reason, her best friend was still quite overly cautious when it came to these sorts of things. So much so that she couldn't clearly remember Millie ever having dated, even though many men had shown a marked interest in her.

"I know, but I just don't think of it that way." Millie's tone was that soft but oh-so-effective reproach that Adele had come to recognize as 'leave me be.' "But now I've agreed to go out with him. Once. I feel I know him well enough—and anyway, it was time."

Adele more than agreed. "I'm so glad! So do you actually like him or are you just being polite?"

Again she didn't seem about to speak.

"You don't have to tell me." Maybe Millie needed that security to thrive more than someone like Adele, who never hesitated to share her feelings, did. "It's all right if it needs to be private until you've figured things out. I won't pressure you."

"That would be nice. But yes. I do like him. Perhaps more than I ought, but we've been good friends for a long time. I think perhaps I have been over-cautious in my desire to not hurry. That, to me, is so sacred, so requiring of depth, and so important to my future. But I expect that there's little I could do to actually convince you that the way I do things makes sense. I feel as if, at last, my theory is proving correct—for this feels right, and I could never have done something that didn't feel right."

Adele sighed. "I'm sorry if I've made you feel that way. Because, Millie, you mean a lot to me—not just as a friend, but as an example of what I could be. Our lives were different, but we lived many of the experiences, and I have had cause to trust in your judgment, for you have never failed me." She fiddled with the phone cord and swallowed. "I know I'm not a good friend to you—"

"Don't say that!" Millie's voice shook. "But don't make me cry right now, for I'm still me—you know I won't use powder or anything."

Adele smirked. "If I were there, I would force you into it."

"Thank heavens you aren't, for he likes me without— or else he wouldn't have asked me out."

"Still—"

"Now, there you go again!" Laughter colored Millie's tone. "You mean well, I know. And I've seen the way you've grown up in past years, so I don't think I fear your bullying in quite the same way."

"Was it bullying?" Adele had expected that some of her words had come off that way, but she hadn't known Millie would think of it that way.

"Hmm ... no. Not exactly. More like I don't have a great deal of fortitude. As we have already established."

"I disagree—you've always stood up to me on the things that matter." Adele glanced over her shoulder at the kitchen table where her family was settling in to eat. "I'd better go, too. Good luck! Call me—even if it's late."

"I'd better not tie up the 'phone lines. I'll call tomorrow night, like always. I'm sure nothing that important will happen. It's just a first date."

"That in itself makes it 'important,' Millie! But I shall wait—albeit impatiently, and eagerly—for what you have to report. Have fun! And don't put too much pressure on yourself or on him. There's time for more than just seeing if you can talk outside of the office."

"Fair enough. And I'm sure I'll survive. Honestly, at my age, not much frightens me. I couldn't have done this at all when I was twenty. Or even twenty-five."

"I think the fact that you're dealing with air raids and all the related horrors might have lessened the terrors caused by a simple night out with a kind man. I'll let you go. Do dress up a little, if you can! I'll talk to you later, Millie."

"All right. Goodbye, Adele."

"Goodbye."

The telephone clinked as she hung it up. Turning back to her family, she sat down for dinner.

After the meal was concluded, she settled Camilla in

for the night and spent some time chatting with Judy and reading to her. She'd rediscovered *The Wind in the Willows* lately, to her great delight. Judy loved it, too, though at first she'd felt it was 'too babyish' for her. Adele thoroughly disagreed. She loved the quaint little tale, personally.

At last it was time for Judy to go to bed. Camilla had been moved out of Adele's room briefly but, finding the nights long and quiet, she'd ended up dragging her crib back.

So she tucked Judy into the nursery—she'd be sleeping there until after Lola found a different place to live, which likely wouldn't happen until Dave came back—and they went over the day and the expectations for tomorrow, which was a nice routine.

There was a kind of steady comfort in it—a beauty to remembering what had been and hoping for what would be. Adele tried to keep it light, and positive, which she wasn't exactly a master at, but at times she could manage it.

"Remember, two weeks until school. It's going to be so much fun!"

Judy's skeptical side-eye glance almost made Adele laugh.

"I know you've been moved around a lot, but you're right where you need to be now. Don't you worry. Remember, I'm good at making friends, so I can give you advice. You just have to keep telling me what's going on." Troy had told her in her recent letter that he wanted her to almost over-emphasize Judy's need to communicate what happened at school. He'd also told Judy privately, apparently, that she should write him any concerns, so between the two, he hoped her transition would be easier than she feared.

"I will." Judy played with the edge of the comforter. "Daddy wants me to tell him, too."

"Right, he mentioned that. He told me he would tell me if it was about keeping you safe, but otherwise, he won't say anything, so you can talk to him." They'd discussed at some length what justified an issue that needed shared and what could be considered a confidence. "But you have to remember it takes a long time for letters to reach him if they do at all."

"That's true." Judy pinched her eyebrows together. "I hadn't thought of that. But I guess they'll get to him if they need to. I think he'll be okay—did I tell you?"

Adele raised her eyebrows. "No, you didn't tell me."

"Yes." She shrugged lightly, as if discussing some small thing. "I think he'll be okay because of God. But even if he's not, he says he'll end up in Heaven anyway, so I can be sad—but not for him. Just for me."

"Right." That made sense, in theory, though Adele wasn't quite ready to accept it. She wanted him to come home—which was a good summary of most of her prayers these days. It didn't seem right for them to get so little time together. Troy deserved far better than that.

Of course not all things about life were fair, nor was her definition of 'fair' an accurate one at times. Perhaps the human concept of just was different than the true one. She just wasn't sure what that was ... yet.

She tucked Judy in, kissed her forehead, and made her way downstairs. Her mother and Lola had already settled into the parlor, each with a book, a routine that Adele found more peaceful than she'd imagined.

Despite the month of the year, a low fire burned in the grate—Lola liked to keep the house warm, sometimes overly so—and the soft crackling of the singular log surrounded by rapidly-diminishing kindling allowed Adele to sink into her novel without much effort.

Outside, rain had started again, and she found herself looking at the front windows where the occasional droplet would be blown against the glass panes.

"It's a beautiful evening," she murmured.

Lola agreed, and Mother told her it was raining, which Adele had to laugh at—because of course she had realized this simple fact. Yet she'd discovered that her mother's observation weren't always meant to point out Adele's flaws but rather to simply start a conversation.

Then she pursued it, and her mother responded in the most unexpected way—sharing a story about a rainy day in Kent when she'd first met Adele's Aunt Ella. Lola added a story about Troy's obsession with charting the weather when he was about fourteen—and Adele loved those insights into his youth. She felt she knew a lot about him as a man and a child, but not as a teenager.

So, the evening slipped on like so many like it—slow, steady, hopeful. There was a rhythm to it that Adele liked, that gave her belief in a better future.

If only, at the end of the war, Troy would come home. That was all that was missing from this scene. Yet it would be a long time, if any newspapers were to be trusted, before the war was over.

*Flowers In Her Heart*

# Part II: Après

"If I hate the sins, I love the sinner, and would
do much for his salvation."

~*The Tenant of Wildfell Hall* by Anne Brontë

# Chapter One

*September 1945*

It was as if every beat of his heart sung the silent refrain: *home, home, home!* He was going home, and nothing else mattered.

Troy Kee took a deep breath as he stepped on to the little station platform. He hoped he'd be able to hail a cab; if not, he had a ten-mile walk ahead of him.

Not that he wasn't used to a march. He'd been hiking thirty miles or more every day for a few years now. He'd gotten used to it.

However, it'd be nice to make this last leg of his journey without breaking a sweat—and in a hurry!

Troy hitched his pack onto his shoulder and

marched over to the ticket booth. A rather large man grinned from behind the counter.

"Where're you off to, young man?"

Troy blinked. He'd not been called 'young man' in years. He was in his late thirties, and that was ancient by army standards. He'd been called 'grandpa,' 'old dad,' and 'Uncle Troy' in turns, but never 'young man.' He smiled.

"Cottage up the way. Hour, two hour walk. I don't suppose you have a quicker way of getting there?" He chuckled. "Can't say I'm not impatient."

The man nodded. "Eh, I can understand that. Though the walk is nice. Is that the house with all the flowers?"

Troy shrugged. "Haven't been there in almost five years, so I'm not quite sure, but I believe so. That sounds like Della."

The ticket booth man cocked his head. "Wife?"

"And two girls to help her plant those flowers—as well as my mother-in-law and sister. And my brother-in-law, when he gets home. He's been in Africa. Now how can I get there?"

"Didn't tell them you're coming home? Surprise?"

Troy bit back an annoyed grunt. "Yes. Now how—"

"How fun for you!"

'Fun' was not the word Troy would use to describe an absence of five years from the only people he loved more than his mustache, but all right then. Whatever this man preferred. "Indeed."

"Let's see now." The man tapped his double chin.

"Next train doesn't come in until the evening. I could drive you up there in my old automobile after my shift is over. Now, granted, it's nothing fancy ... it's probably older than you are."

Troy doubted it—unless it was a prototype of some kind—but he simply smiled and nodded. "That would be wonderful."

He was going home.

It was just as Troy imagined their reunion.

They were out in the garden. Adele had on a big sun hat with ribbons trailing down her back, perfectly manicured nails dipped in the soil as she cleaned early leaves and late weeds from her chrysanthemums and dahlias. She looked lovely, happy, healthy, and perfect.

Judy was nearby, also tending the garden faithfully, and he had to confess he did a double-take when he first laid eyes on her. His baby girl had become a young lady. She must be ... thirteen now? Ridiculous. There were only traces of his tiny daughter there.

He wasn't so familiar with the third person in the garden at the back of their cottage. A little girl with short brunette braids and sparkling brown eyes. She was dancing about, not settled to any one task, all joy and wonder at her surroundings as she scuffed her boots through a pile of early leaves.

*Five. She's five years old, and I've missed almost all*

*of her life so far.*

But that didn't matter anymore. What mattered was that he was home, the war was over, and he was never leaving them again. *Never.*

At last he stepped forward beyond the side gate, letting his reveries slip away. He stopped there when his wife looked up in response to the crunch of his boots on leaves. She sat up then, eyes wide, and her hand came over her mouth as she gasped.

"*Troy.*"

Judy's eyes met his next, and before Adele could move, she was on her feet and racing across the garden to meet him, her strawberry braids flying behind her. He started to bend down to hug her, then realized he didn't need to; her height was almost equalled her mother's.

Amazed and grateful, he held his daughter close for a long moment. He didn't think he could say anything without his voice breaking, so he just held her.

At last, he released her and stepped back, met his Della's eyes. She was grinning—had walked a few steps closer to him, but not all the way, hesitating for God knew what reason.

"Come here!" he said. "Della, darling, come here!"

That recalled her to her senses, and she quickly went into his arms to be hugged and kissed—but the kiss was much, much too brief, and the hug just slightly longer.

She drew away and held a hand out to her youngest, but Camilla hung back, eyes wide. "Camilla, it's your father." Della smiled and motioned her to come forward, but instead she took a step back.

Kellyn Roth

Troy's heart sunk. She didn't recognize him, of course, but he hadn't expected her to be reticent. He'd hoped and prayed she'd be willing to accept him as her father—but he supposed that was too much to ask.

"Oh, don't worry about it, Troy." Della cupped his face with her hand. "She'll warm up to you in a bit." She kissed his cheek. "Oh, and you're awful to come without letting me know you were on your way! I thought I wouldn't see you for another week."

Troy grinned. "I thought it'd be a nice surprise."

"It's the best surprise I've ever gotten." A second hug, a kiss to the other cheek, and she leaned back. "Oh, gosh. Did you know that Lola and Dave are here? And Mother, of course."

Troy raised his eyebrows. "However did Dave get here? I thought things would be slower from Africa than Germany."

"He was wounded just before the war ended— March, I think," Adele said. "Something in his arm, but it got infected. So he got to come home. He's much better now."

"Ah." Troy placed an arm around her shoulders as they walked toward the back door of the house. He wasn't ready to let go of her. He wasn't sure he ever would be ready.

He reached for Judy, and he felt her slip her hand into his. Camilla still wasn't willing to approach him, apparently, but that was all right. Soon she would be ready.

At least, he hoped so. It would be heartbreaking if his

little girl didn't ever get used to him. But he had to believe that she would. Someday. Somehow.

Troy rolled over in bed, confused for a second about his location and the softness of the mattress beneath him, but then he remembered and reached for Adele.

She slid back into his arms, laid her head on his chest, and snuggled in. He sighed. This was what it was supposed to be like. Everything else was insanity; this was normal.

Even if it felt unusual to actually be happy and comfortable and safe.

Some time later, they managed to get out of bed and dressed and downstairs for breakfast. His sister Lola met his eyes in a way that said she had a good idea what they'd been up to until ten in the morning—Troy was usually an early riser, and who knew him better than the woman he'd grown up with?

He chose to ignore her.

After their late breakfast, Troy spent the day catching up with Lola, Dave, and his mother-in-law Mrs. Collier. Judy went to a school in the nearby village while Camilla still didn't want to come near him.

And that was after Adele and Troy had both tried to coax her to sit near him or talk to him or anything.

It broke his heart, and yet he knew better than to push. He'd stand back and let her come to him. Surely she would, eventually.

Everyone had tasks about the house that needed completing, and Troy seemed to be getting in the way of those tasks.

He didn't want to be in the way, but neither did he have anything to do at this present moment besides following Adele around bothering her. Not that she complained—he flattered himself that she'd missed him a bit—but that it bothered him that he had nothing better to do.

He refused to do anything but be with his family for a few weeks, and yet they were already scattering about their lives—the lives they'd formed apart from him.

In particular, Adele was different. Her attitude toward him, her competence around the house, the way she cared for Judy and Camilla, even her interactions with her mother and his sister. It was almost beyond trusting.

It would definitely take some getting used to, and in the meanwhile, it had put him off balance. Granted, if the changes were real—and they must be real—that meant all was well.

Troy just wasn't used to all being well. He was used to holding the family together, his arms trembling under the strain, and suddenly, that was unnecessary. He felt at a loss. Soon he would have some big things to do, but he needed a furlough from active duty—relatively speaking.

Harrington was checking up on things in France to see if it would be all right for Troy to ease on over and ready the vineyard. Until he confirmed that Troy would be safe traveling there, and until certain funds and property were released by the government, there was nothing he could do.

After lunch, Lola waved him into her bedroom, insisting she had something important to discuss. The word 'important' sounded interesting, especially in his present state of mind, so he followed her.

"You'll be the first person I've told other than Dave, and we want to keep it quiet until everything is finalized," she said as she closed the door.

Troy blinked. "What in heaven's name are you talking about, Lola?"

She rolled her eyes. "I'm getting to that!" She grinned. "Troy, Dave and I are adopting a little boy."

He stood still, looking at her for a moment, then smiled and held his arms out to her. She ran over and gave him a big hug.

"Congratulations!" he said. "Do you ... do you feel all right about it now?" His sister had suffered from several miscarriages and difficulties conceiving, and he knew it had been a sensitive subject for many years.

"I do now! The reverend of our church here has been taking in evacuated children as well as helping others who have opened their homes." Lola smiled. "I came to love a lot of those little ones, and when we heard that a five-year-old boy, Harold, would probably go to an orphanage, it seemed like the only option. Dave and I love him. He's a charming little thing."

Troy grinned. She looked so happy now. "When can

we meet him?"

"Soon, I hope! We'll bring him over in a few days. The adoption won't be finalized for a week or so, and then we'll go to London." Lola turned toward the door. "Now, remember, not a word until we're sure we can keep him! But I think it's going to be all right."

"I'm so glad."

And Troy was glad. If anyone deserved happiness, it was his sister.

Adele embraced Lola and then Dave then drew back, verbalizing her congratulations, her excitement, with as much enthusiasm as she could muster.

She was excited for them. She was. It was just that everything in her felt fragile these days, and as such, even her most basic interactions had been reduced to an eggshell walk.

Troy watched her every move like a hawk; she could sense his heart there, on a platter for her to destroy, and he half-expected her to destroy it, too. She realized then that everyone else in this house had seen what it was like for Adele to be a Christian—Troy had not.

It wasn't fair to ask him to trust what he had not seen, when she had never given him the same benefit, but how could she show him? It would take time, time that Adele had thought past. But letters were a poor excuse for the honest proof of day to day faithfulness.

There was only one unspoken promise that ought to be believed—a life.

Yet she could show him. She was determined she could, even if at present it left her preoccupied. She felt nerves, too, skittering about in her stomach, as if she were once again meeting him in that flower shop, ready to be analyzed like all new lovers. Only this time she knew better the stakes—and knew better the rewards for winning his regard.

Hadn't she done that already, though? Or was that just Judy she'd won? She couldn't remember anymore. Surely she had his love, but his respect and admiration would be harder to win.

She shook her head. Half a prayer passed through her mind, and she seized it, added to it, and forced herself into her moment.

"I think you've made the right choice." She glanced between Lola and Dave. "You two will be excellent parents, and it's clear little Harold needs a family. I've seen you with him, Lola, and he is indeed a dear. I can't wait to meet him as my nephew."

Lola nodded eagerly and babbled on about her child, Dave watching her with open affection, and Adele watched them both. She'd become close enough to Lola to be thrilled for her, and seeing her with Dave in these last few months had confirmed Adele's wishes for her own marriage.

She wanted to be that close to Troy. She wanted him to trust her, to believe in her, to be her other half. She wanted to support him and have him support her in the way they were meant to—in the way God intended.

Oh, she'd tried to understand what her role was, but what if she wasn't any good at it? Or what if, perhaps, Troy didn't appreciate what Adele saw as the way a Christian woman ought to behave?

So she watched Lola closely—and Millie, when she saw her—and attended church and in general tried to draw conclusions from the few examples she was given. She wanted to bring some difficult questions before Troy in the next few weeks, and she doubted as to whether she'd be able to do so with any confidence. Particularly, since she'd have to precariously balance submission and a challenge to what he surely wanted to do next.

How could she maintain that balance?

# Chapter Two

Troy pulled Lola close for a moment, patted her back, then released her. She grinned up at him and straightened her jacket and hat slightly. It was a chilly early October morning, and he felt Adele huddle into his side as Lola drew back.

"Remember, we'll be back for Christmas, God willing. Not too far off now."

Dave laughed, adjusting his adopted son on his good arm—the other was still healing in a sling. "It's only a few months off! Can you believe it?"

The train whistled, and steam began issuing from the metal giant at its head.

"I think we'd better board." Lola stood on tiptoes, grabbed Troy's shoulder, and pulled his face down to kiss his cheek. "You behave yourself, Mr. Kee. Adele, don't let him get into more mischief."

"I won't," said Adele. "I hope you're able to settle in London well. You know, getting back to everything."

"I think we will."

"I think I'm ready to get back to banking after all the, shall we say, excitement." Dave Cole jerked his head to the side, lifting the arm in the sling slightly. "Only glad I'm able to slip back into my job. Some fellows won't be so lucky."

Troy agreed. He was having a bit of trouble "slipping back into his job," too. It would seem that a great deal of his money was tied up with the government, and without money, he couldn't get the vineyard back up and running, and without the vineyard up and running, he had no visible means of supporting his wife and children.

One last hug for each of the family members, including a rather stiff one with Mrs. Collier, and Lola followed her husband and son into a compartment. She slid open the window and waved energetically, leaning precariously out, until Dave pulled her back.

Adele stepped away from Troy and picked up Camilla, hoisting the child onto her hip. Honestly, Troy was pleased with how often she picked up her daughter. His Della had always been a rather hands-off parent, and that was putting it nicely. Yet, though Camilla was perfectly capable of walking by herself for any length of time, more often than not, Adele would snuggle Camilla in her arms.

An uneasy feeling in his gut prompted him to wonder what else had changed in the years he'd been gone—more specifically, how his wife had changed. If she was still his Della at the roots.

*But you wanted her to change, to change for the better.* He must remember that. Her letters spoke of the beautiful things God had done to her heart, and it would miraculous. Never would he discount that, even if he wasn't sure what a Christian Adele looked like exactly.

He followed his family to the car. Judy hung back and slid her hand into his. At least he knew Judy hadn't changed, even if Adele might have. Judy was approaching womanhood, yes, but she was still his baby girl. He sensed she still wasn't quite ready to have a long conversation with him, but even talking was intimate to Judy. Troy understood needing to hang back and make sure he was still hers—which he was, of course. He'd always be hers, whenever she wanted him.

They drove home, and Camilla dashed off to play with her favorite dolls while Judy had some studying to do for an important test. He'd never really known Judy as an active student, due to all their moving around, and it was almost strange to think about.

"So what's next for you?" Adele asked.

Troy blinked. Had he not mentioned it? "What do you mean?"

"I mean, you can't just hang about the house doing nothing!" Adele laughed and walked before him into the parlor. "I'm usually the one who has no plans. I'm surprised you're not already up to something."

Troy's brow wrinkled. "I *am* already up to something."

"What is that?" She took a seat on the sofa and patted the place beside her. "I guess we ought to discuss it."

"Yes." He sat down next to her. "But I thought you knew—Della, we're going to France next month." That had always been the plan as far as he was concerned. England was just a stopping point.

She stared at him blankly for a moment before responding. "But the vineyard isn't up and running. I thought you said your finances were tied up, too."

Troy nodded. "Yes, but that doesn't mean we can't go home."

She winced, and it occurred to Troy that she'd spent only a bit over a year at the vineyard since their remarriage and perhaps didn't consider it home as he did. Despite that wince, though, her response was milder than he'd expected. "Are you sure we should take Judy out of school mid-term? She's just starting to open up to making friends, and there's even a boy she's expressed some interest in, and—"

His heart jumped, and his fists clenched. "*What?*"

"Perhaps I shouldn't have told you that." She smiled, appearing somewhat bemused. "Yes, she has a bit of a crush on this Larry fellow a class ahead of her."

"But she's thirteen!" Restless, he stood, though he wasn't really sure what action he wanted to take. Perhaps finding said Larry fellow and giving him a good yelling at? That might be extreme, but Troy wanted to do it nevertheless.

"Oh, come on, Troy, don't tell me you never had a crush when you were her age! I know I had half a dozen." She patted the seat beside her. Everything about her reminded him that she wasn't afraid, well, of anything. Where had she gotten that confidence? He'd left a woman wobbling about like a newborn foal. "Sit down!"

"I will not! This is all the more reason to leave for France as soon as possible."

"Troy!" Adele reached for his hand and tugged him down. "Now, you be quiet for a moment and let me talk." She cupped his chin with her hand and forced him to look at her. "Judy is a shy, quiet girl, and I know it's hard for her to make friends. But now she's got a few girls she seems to at least have a civil relationship with, and given the fact that when she's alone with me, she talks of nothing but, 'Larry, Larry, Larry,' I think it's fair to assume that he's also a friend."

"But—"

"But what, Troy? It's an innocent crush; it's not doing anyone any harm. Besides, I think it's good for her."

"Romance is almost never good for anyone!"

She laughed again as if he was joking, but he wasn't. Every sane choice he'd made hadn't involved emotions. Didn't Adele remember that he'd almost lost her because of rampant feelings? But perhaps she didn't think of it that way.

"I don't know if I'd call it romance," she said when she'd recovered sufficiently to speak. "She won't remember who he was in a year, which is not my idea of romance. But that doesn't change the fact that she's growing up, and perhaps she needs a safe environment to do so—one where she can actually speak the language she's being taught in, for one."

He scrunched up his shoulders defensively and set his jaw. "She tells me she's coming along in her French lessons."

"Yes, but 'coming along' in French means she might be able to introduce herself and have a lively discussion on various items in the room with her schoolmates, which I don't consider to be exactly comforting. Yes, she's picked up enough to get on if she were traveling or to understand a basic conversation, but she's not proficient yet. As shy as she is, she won't speak until she's fluent. I just think we should give her a few more months. Would you consider that?"

Troy wasn't sure what to think of that. He'd always assumed they would settle in and be quite the natural family in France, but Adele seemed to think it would be hard for Judy—and the way she was talking, it would be hard for his wife, too.

"France is our home. There's nothing for me in England." No occupation, no reason to stay, no *life*.

"It doesn't feel like home, though. That is, it doesn't to me, and it can't to Judy. I … I think she would tell you she wanted to go, but I don't think she'd feel it. Of course it won't matter so much for Camilla, except leaving her Granny and aunts, but it will hurt to be so far away from family. I know Lola and Millie don't live here, but London is close enough to visit or to have them visit us.

If we were in France ..." Adele's voice trailed off, but the thought continued in Troy's head.

"But that doesn't change the fact that my job, our livelihood, exists in France."

Her lips pressed together. "Couldn't you manage things from here?"

"Couldn't you learn to give up yourself for one solid minute?"

She stared at him then, silent, and guilt stole its way into his soul. He shouldn't have said that. It wasn't fair to speak words in frustration and disappointment that could hurt her, especially given that she was trying so hard to be a faithful wife and mother. It wasn't as if it came naturally to her, and yet she put out a solid effort every day.

But Adele wanted him to do something impossible—she wanted him to give up his dreams of a life where he could have a wife and children in the only home he'd known since he was eleven years old, the home he had created from his teens to be a place for his family.

He couldn't.

In time, she replied softly. "I don't believe I'm being selfish, Troy. I love you, but I love the girls, too, and I'm trying to show you how difficult it would be for them, as well as myself, to make this transition immediately."

He took her hand and squeezed it. "I appreciate your effort."

"But it's not enough, is it? You need us to go to France." Her voice had an edge to it, and he knew she was forcing the words out.

"I ... I don't know. No. I suppose not." He put his arm around her shoulders and hugged her. "It's hectic in France now, anyway."

He heard her sigh of relief. "Good. Let's at least wait until after the Christmas holidays, dear." She kissed his cheek then stood. "You're an angel, you know. Thank you for understanding."

Understanding? Oh, he understood—that he might lose her if he continued this vein of conversation. It was easier to give up than to fight her.

He'd listened to her.

As she returned to her normal routines—preparing lunch, chatting with Camilla and her mother—she felt gratitude flowing through her. Perhaps he believed in her more than she thought.

There was hope for her marriage. Yes, there was— shining hope erasing her doubts. Her prayers had been answered, for Troy believed in her.

What more could she ask? He'd only been back a few weeks, and already, he'd respected her wishes about something that could by no means be easy for him.

This, of course, made her love him even more. She was careful to be affectionate and open to him that evening, tempering her reactions to some of his silliness, guarding her tongue when she might have made comments about his somewhat gloomy attitude. Since he had sacrificed so much for her and their daughters, she wanted to make his life as easy as possible. Though, of course, he was due her love regardless of how he behaved.

Love, if not gifted rather than bargained for, was a worthless treasure.

Judy was at school, which left Troy even less to do than before. Never mind that his head was filled with make-believe images of this "Larry" fellow. Plotting revenge on a fourteen-year-old for crimes he hadn't committed wasn't exactly a worthwhile occupation.

Of course, Adele was busy. Besides gardening, she'd also made friends in a nearby village and gotten involved in some social club type things. He would've found it amusing if he didn't wish she'd stay home and at least give him someone to talk to.

But usually he was good at self-entertaining, even when he really had nothing to do, so he supposed it was partially stubbornness that made him so restless.

He was stubbornly restless.

As he sat at the kitchen table, his eyes drifted to the window. Camilla was out there, collecting and piling leaves—not with a rake, as one was expected to do, but with her hands.

It was amusing to say the least. Her enthusiasm was unbarred by the slowness of proceedings, and she raced about eagerly, adding to her colorful collection.

Adele had kept her youngest out of school an extra term, though he felt that was as much to keep Camilla to herself as anything. He understood the impulse—and was grateful for it.

Still Camilla wouldn't talk to him. Troy sighed at the thought. She seemed an exuberant, happy little girl, crawling into her mother or Granny's lap, playing with Judy, and asking lots of questions about practically everything. However, she'd yet to warm up to Troy, and he'd been the recipient of more than one scathing glare when he'd attempted to chat with her.

He just wanted to be friends with his daughter. Was that so much to ask? Apparently so. But he wouldn't push; he'd let her come to him. That, he felt, was the way to begin a relationship—on her ground, not his.

Yet he supposed he could try and see if he were welcome one last time. He stood, grabbed his jacket from the hook by the door, and walked out into the chilly autumn morning.

Camilla's head immediately snapped up at the creak of the back door, and when she saw him, her eyes narrowed. She returned to her collection and sat on it, gathering the leaves about her protectively.

"Hello, Camilla. Would you like some help?"

She didn't reply.

"You know," he said, "I can think of a way to gather the leaves a lot more efficiently."

She didn't seem impressed, though it was hard to tell as she refused to make eye contact with him.

"Wouldn't you like a friend?"

That got her attention. She turned to him, hands folded across her chest and jaw set firmly. It was adorable, but he didn't laugh. "Already got a friend."

"Judy?" Troy suggested.

Camilla shook her head emphatically. "No. She's my sister."

"Can't she be both?"

"*No.*"

"Ah. Then who is your friend?"

"Amy."

*Amy, Amy* … Troy searched his mind. He couldn't seem to remember Adele mentioning the name in any of her letters, though she'd never been particularly detailed in them. Adele wasn't one to wax on.

"Does Amy live in the village?" he asked at last.

"No."

He raised his eyebrows. "Where does she live?"

"Here."

Troy blinked. "Oh."

"She stays in my room," Camilla continued, "and we do everything together. She became my friend when my dog died. He came from France when I was a baby, and his name was Holt, and he was yellow. Now he's under the garden. But I have Amy. So I don't need a friend."

"Ah." So Amy was some sort of imaginary companion? A replacement for Troy's dog, Holt, who had passed of old age last year? That must be it. Interesting. "What's wrong with having two friends? I have more than one friend. I have Harrington and your

207

mother and Judy. Could you be friends with Amy *and* me?"

Camilla cocked her head. "I think Amy might be jealous."

"Why don't you ask her?" Troy suggested.

Camilla turned from him and whispered softly to herself, and Troy held his breath until she turned back to him.

"She says it's okay. As long as we can all be friends together."

Troy shrugged. "I'm fine with that if you are."

"I am."

"Okay, then. Shall we gather some more leaves?"

Camilla glanced down at her leaf pile then back to Troy. "I don't think Amy and I want to gather leaves. But ..." A slight grin. "If you'll come with us, we can go down to the brook. We can't go alone, but we can go if we have a grownup. And you're a grownup. Aren't you?"

Troy nodded. "I am a grownup. But why do you want to go down to the brook?"

"Because it's pretty," Camilla said. "I like playing there." She marched over to him and held out her hand. He took it, marveling at the smallness of it as they walked out of the side gate together.

He'd been right; the stream was back in the crop of trees behind the cottage, not far away. It wasn't particularly deep, save a few particular spots, but it was wide and slow and lazy, even given the bursts of rain they'd been having recently.

Camilla grinned up at him and tugged his hand,

urging him to a place where the bank flattened into a pebbled beach, no more than a few yards wide and not much longer, but still enough room for a girl and her father—and her friend Amy—to stand.

"This is me and Amy's favorite place." Camilla cocked her head. "It can be yours, too, now."

"Okay," said Troy.

"We like to make rock castles, and throw pebbles in and watch them sink, and put leaves and twigs to sail. We like to think they go all the way to the ocean." Camilla glanced up at him. "Have you been to the ocean?"

"Yes," Troy said. "My home is right by the sea, actually."

"Oh." Camilla wrinkled her brow. "Mommy says your home is here. Or, at least, she says you're going to live here now for a while."

"Yes. I'll live with you anywhere. We're a family."

Camilla narrowed her eyes. "How come we weren't a family before?"

Troy offered what he felt must be a weak smile. At least, it seemed to shake his lips in a rather unmanly way. "Because of the war." How he hated the war.

"Oh." Camilla's expression lightened. "That makes sense. Lots of dads had to be in the war, didn't they?"

"Yes."

She turned toward the water then glanced over her shoulder at him. "Do you like being a family again?"

"More than anything in the world." That wasn't something he had to think about.

She nodded. "Good."

"Do ... do you like my being a part of the family again, Camilla?"

She picked up a twig with a brilliant crimson leaf attached to it, walked to the edge of the brook, and set it to float. "I don't know. Mommy always *said* you'd come home, but I wasn't sure you would since I didn't know anything about you. Judy has your picture, and Mommy has some more in a book. But it was hard to think of the picture being a real daddy, you know. Besides, none of my book friends have any fathers—at least, most of them don't. Mary in *The Secret Garden* is an orphan. I think I'd like to be one, and to have a friend with a fox cub."

Troy was unfamiliar with that story, so he just said, "Ah." He walked to her side. "Do you think you'll get used to me?"

"I think so. Especially if we're friends." A long silence. "But it's hard because Mommy has been here as long as I can remember, and Judy, and Granny, and Auntie Lola, and Auntie Millie always came to visit, but ... I never did have you until now. Did you ever even see me?"

"I did." Troy sighed. "I was here when you were born, and I was here when you were a few months old. So I know you a bit, even if you don't know me. And your mother wrote to me about you. Your first steps, your first word ..." His voice trailed off as the unfairness of it all settled on him.

He'd wanted to have a family. When he was young, being a husband and father had been a foreign and strange idea—but as he became an adult, the idea grew on him until it was all he wanted.

Then, between the divorce and the war, he didn't get to see either of his baby girls learn to walk and talk; he didn't get to be a part of their first memories. He would never see a child of his grow from infancy to toddlerhood, from toddlerhood to childhood.

He'd even missed crucial years of Judy's life, though he didn't intend to miss another one ever again. She wasn't exactly a woman, but in a few years, she would be a young lady, and even now she was getting crushes and acting like a teenager. It was disturbing, and it had been a rude awakening for him rather than a gradual change.

But Troy wouldn't go blaming the world for his misfortunes. First, because missing Judy's first years had been as much his mistake as Adele's, and second, because he didn't regret serving his country. Still, it did feel dashed unfair.

He turned his attention back to the present and a five-year-old girl who wanted to get to know her new friend.

# Chapter Three

The telephone rang, and Adele answered it. Based on the fact that she resolutely pretended not to understand the person on the other end, and then proceeded to make several fakely flirtatious remarks, Troy guessed it was Harrington.

He walked over to her, and she handed the receiver over. Harrington was even more grouchy than usual, and he got straight to the point.

"You can come. I've got the money straightened out, and the vineyard's fine. We have a lot of work to do to get it back into working order, but I'm not afraid of hard work. When will you be here?"

So that was it. He would definitely be moving his

family to France, whether Adele liked it or not. And she wouldn't like it, but God help him, he hoped she'd go along despite her dislike for the idea.

He had to make this decision for them. A man didn't marry a woman and then live separately from her, or live in the place of her choosing if the place of her choosing was away from his job. There needed to be solidarity, and he hoped she'd see that.

Or at least pretend to.

*God, don't let my marriage be broken again— please. I'm not to say what happens in my life, but I know it would be impossible to come back from that again. For Judy and Camilla ... don't let there be strife. Let it resolve itself easily.*

He placed the receiver in its cradle and turned to walk to the back of the cottage where the kitchen was located.

His hand was on the doorknob, and he was taking the breath which would carry the words to Della's ears, when Camilla's voice broke the silence from behind the door.

"Went to the brook with Daddy yesterday."

The regular *chop, chop* of vegetables being mutilated ceased. "Is that so?" Adele's voice was filled with a kind of gentle wonder he'd never heard in her before.

"Yep." There was a silence, and he presumed that Camilla had no further thoughts to voice on the subject.

"And ... did you have a good time?" Della prompted.

"Yes. Amy and I like him a lot, you know. He's our friend."

"Oh, good." Adele was probably afraid to say anything more—Troy could understand that. He didn't want to break the spell and scare her off. But if he and Camilla could love each other, that would be nothing short of perfection.

"We're going on another adventure soon," Camilla said. "Amy wants to."

"Oh? Have you told Daddy about this adventure?"

"No. But he'll want to come. He likes spending time with Amy and me."

"Yes, I think he does."

Troy leaned back from the door, thinking. He wondered if the move would endanger his relationship with Camilla. He thought, perhaps, before he made any major changes, he needed to make sure his foundation was firm.

That his family was firm. That they could move as one, literally and figuratively.

Troy sighed and walked back to the telephone. In no time, Harrington's deep, grumbly voice answered.

"It's Troy. I need some more time," he said. "I can't move the girls to France until ... Anyway, I want to take a few months or at least a few more weeks to get them used to me again."

There was a long silence before Harrington replied. "You're soft, Troy."

He grinned wryly. "I am."

"I'll see you in six months, then."

Troy laughed. "It won't be that long, Harrington."

He grunted and hung up.

Troy mumbled under his breath as he set the receiver down.

Troy took Camilla's hand in his as they walked out of the back door and through the garden. Judy moved to his other side as they walked toward the brook in the woods behind the cottage.

At last, they arrived at the bank of the creek. It was a rainy day, and rather chilly, but Adele had a bad headache—and Adele wasn't the type of woman who pretended illness she didn't truly feel—so Troy had agreed to get everyone out of the house save Mrs. Collier who wasn't much of a noisemaker.

However, the best he could think to do was go for a walk to the creek. Oddly enough, Judy had seemed somewhat enthused about this. He'd thought she'd roll her eyes and drag her heels, as befit a thirteen-year-old. But he supposed he didn't know thirteen-year-old Judy very well, so perhaps she was just the type of girl who actually liked to spend time with her father and little sister.

He hoped so. That was the type of girl he wanted her to be. Caring and loving, even if it was blasted difficult growing up—which it was. In fact, he often thought it was more difficult for girls than for boys.

At least, it'd been tougher for Lola than him. However, Lola hadn't had a mother while Troy had made do with Harrington as a father, so it could also be a matter of not having the proper guidance. He wasn't sure which.

"Daddy, what'll we do now?" Camilla asked when they reached the little beach area which she called her special spot.

"What would you and Amy and Judy like to do?" Troy asked.

"I don't know." Camilla squinted for a moment. "I think Amy would like to ... to play in the stream?" She glanced hesitantly up at Troy, and he furrowed his brow.

It wasn't really a good idea. After all, it was quite cold, and the rain was coming down, and they really needed to keep at least nominally clean and dry.

But Camilla's eyes pleaded with him, and there was a subtle interest in Judy's. "All right," said Troy. "I don't see what it hurts ..." He'd never caught his death of cold from playing in a brook yet, and the girls were probably equally as hearty. There was no need to worry. "As long as we don't—"

Camilla dived forward into the stream, splashing up to her knees in the water and shrieking at the cold. "Come on, Daddy!"

He laughed, but unlike Camilla, he paused to remove his shoes and socks and roll up his trousers before following his daughter into the brook.

Judy hesitated on the bank, staring at them as if they were insane, but eventually she too removed her shoes and followed them in.

Troy picked Camilla up around the waist and

resolutely removed her shoes and socks and tossed them on the bank. They were soaked already, yes, but it would be best if they got at least a little time to dry.

Though Adele was probably going to throw a fit either way.

The three adventurers—and Amy—arrived back at the cottage dripping wet and shivering, but laughing all the same. Adele met them at the door.

"Troy!" She smothered her laughter, hands on hips. Thankfully, her headache from earlier had largely dissipated leaving behind only fragile remnants—slight nausea and an ache in her bones that led her to believe she might be getting a light flu. "What on earth—?"

Troy was grinning like an idiot. "Playing in the brook." He set Camilla down just inside the door. "Feeling better?"

"Lots, but look at you three! Now, let's just hope none of you catch a head cold."

Troy chuckled. "Ah, we're stronger than that, Della dear. We'll just get a bit unfrozen, have some hot cocoa and tea, and we'll be good as new!"

Adele shook her head, but she gathered them in and stripped Camilla while Judy ran up to her room for a change of clothes. Troy went to change into a fresh pair of trousers, but his shirt hadn't gotten wet—just his coat—so he was all right in that concern. Camilla, of course, required an entirely new outfit, but just this once, Adele didn't mind. She was grateful her daughter and husband were finally bonding.

In no time at all, Troy, Adele, Judy, Camilla, and Mother—who'd come down to help get the kitchen mopped—settled in the kitchen with warm drinks.

There was an easy camaraderie amongst them now. Adele found herself looking around the group and smiling to herself like an idiot. She was unable to explain her exact reasoning when Troy questioned her, but certainly he felt it, too. Despite his uneasiness about staying in England for a few months, it was the right decision for them.

At last, they were beginning to thrive.

Millie drove down from London a week later with her husband of three years, Lennon Young, and her young daughter, Erin. Though Millie had been Adele's best friend since they were seven years old, Troy hadn't seen her in years, and of course had never met her husband.

Lennon turned out to be a pleasant sort, and Troy didn't mind chatting with him. He was in politics, sort of, or at least his primary job had been in the war office. He had a bad leg and walked with a limp from a farming accident in his boyhood.

Actually, Troy soon learned, Lennon had been

Millie's superior for years, asking her out many times in the last decade, and she'd only agreed about three months before they became engaged.

There was something to knowing one's spouse a long time before marriage. He often wished he'd taken time with Adele, really gotten to know her, before committing. They had been too hasty.

But if he hadn't committed then, they might not have gotten married—probably wouldn't have—and he wouldn't have Judy and Camilla. So he didn't regret his decisions, exactly, though he would tell others to dedicate more time to their relationships before throwing themselves into a lifelong bond with a person.

Committing to children, committing to teamwork, committing to love and trust and respect for a lifetime. It took more guts and less sentimentalism than novels and movies alike proclaimed, and Troy knew now that it was wise to make sure the person you chose was absolutely right.

Adele whisked Millie off to her bedroom for a one-on-one chat as soon as she'd arrived, and Judy took charge of Erin, leading her and Camilla out to play in the garden. Lennon and Troy chatted about politics and jobs and what they'd all be doing after the war.

"So will you stay in London?" Troy asked.

"Actually, no. I'm quitting my job, and of course Millie is, and we're moving to the country." Lennon grinned. "May seem foolish, given that we have Erin's well-being to worry about, but we have enough savings to go off for about two years if we really needed to, and we want to raise her in the country, so it just makes sense. I'm sure I can find a job—if not, I can probably find something in London that will let me commute. Though I'd rather not."

Troy nodded slowly. He'd feel much the same way if he lived in the city. He honestly couldn't imagine living in all the noise, traffic, and bustle. Too complicated for his taste.

"Where are you going?"

Lennon rubbed his chin. "Our first choice was Creling in Kent—that's where her parents live—and we'd actually found a house there, but the deal fell through. It's busy in Creling now, anyway—it's becoming quite the center of traffic. Right between Dover and London, I suppose. It's a lovely place with some old houses and mansions, and it's become a tourist destination. So now we're looking around again. Millie's parents might move out of Creling, anyway—they want somewhere quieter, and her sisters have left home now, so there's not much there for them."

Troy nodded. That made sense.

Adele came running down the stairs just then. "Troy! Did you hear that they're moving to the country?"

"Lennon told me."

"Oh." She grinned. "Isn't it wonderful?"

"I don't see why. I mean, I suppose so?" Troy wasn't sure how to respond to her enthusiasm. Nothing wrong with moving to the country, and he approved, but "wonderful" was a decidedly strong word.

"I think Millie and Lennon should move here and

live close to us! It would be amazing. Like a childhood dream."

Troy's heart stopped. *Live near us?* But they weren't going to live in England. They were going to live in France. They must. It was their home. There was no other way.

Adele left before he could address her further, and this was hardly the time, but he knew he must—and he dreaded that conversation.

# Chapter Four

After Millie and her family had left, Troy told Adele he needed to speak with her. He honestly wasn't sure what he needed to say, only that it was time to put his foot down.

This wasn't their home. France was their home! It always had been. He'd brought her there as his bride, brought her back after their remarriage ... Judy had been born there, and Camilla would have been if not for the war.

Everything about their life would have existed there if not for the war.

He was trying not to be bitter, but it seemed unfair

that one man should have to live through two such major conflicts in the space of his lifetime. Yes, he had only been a child during the Great War, but losing his parents and being uprooted from his home had left a mark he still wasn't sure he'd managed to rub out. Only Harrington and Lola had gotten him through those terrible years, and he'd felt incomplete, lost for much of his young adulthood.

Even now, he wasn't sure he was quite normal.

And having to experience the same things his father had experienced in the weeks and months leading up to his death made it even more difficult. Ground it into his mind without fail.

Troy knew the war needed to be fought, the evil had needed to be destroyed, and good—for he truly believed he had fought on the good side—must triumph.

Yet at such a cost to all the men who fought for either side. Yet such a scar left on his soul and so many other souls. Yet at such an expense to his family and his life.

He'd considered himself one of the lucky ones. He'd come home in one piece, physically, save a bit of fading exhaustion, and he was alive. There was so much to be thankful for.

But that didn't change the fact that he was still picking up the pieces from his ruined life. That didn't change the fact that his wife had changed her mind about living at his home—or that's what it felt like. It felt like she didn't want to be near him.

After all, she knew he must live near his work, didn't she? Surely she did. She knew how involving it was. Even if he hired others to do jobs for him, which he almost always did, someone needed to be there to oversee, to help out, to make sure everything ran as smoothly as could be.

So he turned to Adele with a twisted face and a heavy heart. She'd sat down on the edge of the bed, hands folded in her lap, and was looking at him oddly.

"Is something wrong, Troy?" Her voice was soft, and there was no stubbornness or malice in her tone or face. No, she didn't realize. She hadn't even thought of it. And he'd have to try to be as gentle as he could. She deserved that gentleness. She deserved the knowledge that he would take good care of her.

But at the same time, he had to make this decision for the family.

"Della ..." He reached up and rubbed the back of his neck. "Della, you know I love you very much, don't you?"

Hesitation flashed across her face, no doubt at the fact that he'd chosen to remind her of this in such an awkward way. "I know," she replied. "I just ... what's going on, Troy?"

"Nothing, nothing." Troy sighed then stepped forward and took a seat next to her. "I lied. There is something ..."

Her brow furrowed. "What is it?"

"I know you'd like to stay in England, Della, but we can't. We need to move to France. And I know it's going to be difficult for you and the girls, but we must. There's no other way. I need to be there, and I need you to be at my side, and of course the girls must be there, too. And it's not because I … I don't want you to have whatever you want to have, but it's because I love you and want to be near you." His voice trailed off.

Her face was rather emotionless, but not cold. She took his hand. "Are you okay, Troy? You're shaking."

"Maybe a bit." He chuckled awkwardly. "I can't help but think you're going to yell at me. I can't help but think that maybe, just maybe … you won't want to be with me on my terms. That I can only be your husband if … if things are going your way."

She blinked. "Did I ever say that?"

"No, but I always thought you felt that way. I know you do like to get your way …"

"Troy!" She was laughing at him now. Her hand came up and cupped his face. "Darling, you're not going to lose me over this. I promise you that." She kissed him, then drew back. "Look at me. I'm not leaving you! I'm never leaving you again. I love you, all right? I do."

"I know you love me, but it's hard to believe it, Della, sometimes. Especially when you've evinced hesitance to do what we need to do … which is move to France."

"Ah." She cocked her head. "Do we really need to? I thought you just wanted to." She laid her head against his shoulder. "How soon?"

It was his turn to stare, not understanding, at her. "You mean … you mean you don't intend to … You are all right with moving to France?"

"Yes. Of course. If that's where you need us to go." She sighed. Troy could feel the defeat in her posture. This wasn't what she wanted, not really.

He should be happy now. But he wasn't. He wanted *her* to be happy. "Della?" he whispered.

"Hmm?"

"What if we could spend most of the year in France—and holidays in England. We could keep the house open for your mother, and you could visit from time to time as you like, even on the occasional long weekend."

She pushed back and looked up at him, as if afraid he was joking.

He smiled at the light in her eyes. "I know how much it means to you to live with your mother. I know you've started to have a decent relationship. Then for part of the year, at least, you could live near Millie and her family. Would you like that?"

"Oh, Troy!" She wrapped her arms around him then, tight, and buried her face in his shoulder. "Could we do that?"

"Of course, darling!"

"We wouldn't exactly need two homes. This could just be my mother's home—it's not like she can't afford to maintain it—and we could visit often. But as long as we could come to England and see our family ..."

"We'll work it out." Troy hugged her close. "I'm glad you're not angry with me."

"Of course I'm not." She leaned back. "Troy, I promise you, even though it's probably difficult for you to realize sometimes, that I love you. I'll love you ... I'll love you forever. I want to do my best to be a good wife and mother. I sometimes fail, but I do my best."

He didn't know what to say; he just held on to her.

"I do have one small request, though." She tipped her head back.

"What?"

"Could the girls and I stay in England for a bit longer? Until … I don't know how you'll feel about this, but until next summer."

Troy blinked. That was indeed something he wasn't sure how he felt about. He wanted to please her, but on the other hand, that was a long time to wait. "Wouldn't Christmas be better, darling? Judy could finish up her term that way, and we could still get some time to adjust."

Adele shook her head. "There's a special reason why I'd like to wait until July. Darling, I'm going to have a baby."

"Wh-what?"

"And I'd like to have it near my mother and Millie, if you don't mind—at the hospital where we had Camilla. It was so nice there."

His heart stopped. "A baby?"

"Yes, I think in June, which is why I'd like to wait until then."

"But … I thought you said Camilla was the absolute last."

Adele laughed. "I guess I was wrong."

# Chapter Five

*August 1946*
*French Riviera*

As the car drew up the long drive between rows of grapes, Troy reached for his wife and put an arm around her shoulders. She smiled up at him. There was bravery in those brown eyes that he'd never seen before—but he supposed they needed to be brave.

France was going to take some time to recover from the scars of the war, and Troy wasn't sure how long it would take for things to heal. But they would, eventually. They *must*.

"Things don't seem so bad here." Judy, who sat in

the back, seemed at least somewhat cheerful.

"No, darling. And soon everything will be back to normal."

"Pretty!" Camilla squealed as a view of the Mediterranean swept before them around a bend.

From the front seat, on the other side of Adele, Harrington grunted. "You get used to it. And then you stop exclaiming over it and being annoying."

"Hey, don't talk to my daughter that way," Troy said, but he was laughing inside. Harrington might pretend he hated children, but in no time at all, he'd be in love with Camilla—and with Troy's son.

Kenny began fussing in Della's arms.

"We're almost home," Troy said by means of consoling his son. "Just around the bend, and we're home."

At last they caught sight of the house. Troy let out a sigh of relief. That was his home, his misshapen chateau that had belonged to his eccentric uncle before him.

He parked the car, stepped out, and turned to reach for Mr. Kenneth Millard Kee. "There's my boy." Troy stepped back, adjusting his arms around him. "No need to fuss. We'll get you down for a nice nap in a minute."

Adele got out of the car and adjusted the strap of one of her thirty-three purses against her shoulder. "Assuming he'll go down."

"I think he's tired," Troy said.

"Tired is one thing—willing to sleep quite another." But she smiled around the dark circles under her eyes. At least she was smiling—traveling with a month-old baby was exhausting.

"I'm sure we'll get him down. If you want, I can even take care of him and let you nap." Troy grinned. "That is, if the bedrooms are in any sort of order. Harrington, did you get the bassinet out of the attic?"

"I'm not completely incompetent in my old age," Harrington rebuked. But Troy knew the gruffness was just his way of welcoming his family home. At least temporarily. They'd be spending parts of the holidays and most summers in England, or at least Adele and the children would.

As Mrs. Collier grew more elderly, Troy imagined the visits would be more frequent, but since Millie and Lennon had managed to secure a house near the Kees' cottage and agreed to keep an eye on her, as well as bring their daughter over to visit, Troy imagined his mother-in-law wouldn't get too lonely. Mrs. Collier was an independent woman, anyway.

"Now to get unpacked." Troy realized that holding a baby might hinder the unloading a bit, but thankfully Judy was on hand to take Kenny and whisk him and Camilla into the house to do some exploring. She even kept him pacified with soft pats and carefully-placed arms. Troy had soon learned that his fourteen-year-old daughter was a champion with babies, and she adored her little brother.

At last everything was unloaded, and Adele took Kenny up to their bedroom—supposedly to give them both a nap. After seeing that Judy and Camilla were well-occupied, Troy followed, thinking Adele might need some help getting their son down. Kenny could be a bit rambunctious.

However, he found them both tucked into the bed, Kenny cuddled against Adele's chest, fast asleep. He smiled and adjusted the covers over them. His wife, his son, and two daughters downstairs—as well as Harrington. A family. A real family.

He went to his briefcase, which he'd set on the ground of his bedroom when he was unloading, and opened it. Out came his most treasured possession, which had gone everywhere with him for fifteen years now.

A photograph of his Della from the early days of their marriage. Head thrown back in laughter, eyes dancing at him, love for the man behind the camera—him—in her eyes.

He set the frame on the bedside table and stepped back to admire it. Perfect. Now, he felt, it had a permanent resting place. Now he wouldn't have to move it around.

He'd finally brought his lady of the vineyard home, and now she could reign here. Now he could be content.

Leaving the framed photograph on the table, he tiptoed out of the room to let them sleep.

# A Note to the Reader

Welcome to the section of the book that I cannot guarantee you read. I always read any kind of material the author writes at the end of the book, though, so I decided I would write it anyways.

I pray this novel blessed you, but if it didn't, no worries. Post a review either way!

This book is one I wrote directly after finishing my first-ever novel (which is part of a completely different series, The Chronicles of Alice and Ivy). I never expected it to become a series (it ended up being book 2 after some revisions), nor did I expect it to be longer than a short story.

However, here I am, with this full-length novel being published.

The idea for this story originally bloomed out of *The Parent Trap* and *GiGi*. Basically, I wanted to play with the idea of a divorced couple and the complicated situation their separation left behind for their child.

Obviously, it has expanded a lot since then. However, you may remember, if you have followed me since the beginning of my author journey, that several different editions of this novel have been out. The first version ever was launched in September 2016—so many years ago!

Though so many things have changed about the novel, the

core story has remained the same: an exploration of family, of second chances, of sacrificing selfishness for the sake of those you love. Adele was heavily inspired by the arc of the main characters in *The Bird in the Tree* by Elizabeth Goudge, an excellent and under-appreciated novel.

God bless you & keep you—may He make His face shine upon you—may the Lord lift up His countenance upon You and give You peace.

Kellyn Roth
April 2022
White Salmon, WA

www.ingramcontent.com/pod-product-compliance
Lightning Source LLC
Chambersburg PA
CBHW030111260626
47156CB00008B/2614